S0-EAO-659

THE TRAVELERS

PRESENT IN THE PAST

BY ELAINE SCHMIDT

THE TRAVELERS: PRESENT IN THE PAST

BY ELAINE SCHMIDT

Edited by Diane McLendon
Book designed by Bob Deck
Cover illustration by Neil Nakahodo

All rights reserved.

Copyright © 2012 The Kansas City Star Co. and Elaine Schmidt

No part of this book may be reproduced, stored in a retrieval system, or transmitted in any form or by any means electronic, mechanical, photocopying, recording or otherwise, without the prior consent of the publisher.

Published by Kansas City Star Books.

First edition. First printing.

Paperback ISBN: 978-1-61169-068-2
E-book ISBN: 978-1-61169-069-9
Library of Congress Number: 2012948376

Printed in the United States of America by Walsworth Publishing Co., Marceline, Missouri.

To order copies, call 816-234-4636 and say "BOOKS."

DEDICATION

Although this book is a work of fiction, it was inspired by the spirited journal and exquisitely stitched quilt created by Winnie Longenecker during the late 1800s. Her quilt, which she stored in a hope chest to be used in her home when she married, has been carefully passed through generations of her family to the present day, along with her journal and a quilt made by her mother. Reading Winnie's journal, I felt as though I got to know her and her world. I wondered what she might have thought of our world today. That wondering became this book.

Writing a book may be a solitary experience, but polishing it is a team effort. Heartfelt thanks to my first reader, Kristin Strunk, and my subsequent readers, Linda Jaeger, Marie Mouser, Julie Bayard, Laura Bayard, Holly Wilinski and Maddie Wilinski. Thanks to my mother-in-law, Judy Jones, who first put Winnie's journal in my hands, and Edith Long, who entrusted me with Winnie's quilt. Thanks to my mother, Helen Paul, for reading an early incarnation of the book, but more significantly for instilling in me a life-long love of reading. My deepest thanks to my husband, Mark Hoelscher, whose constant encouragement and support convinced me to sit down and write this story in the first place.

CHAPTER I

Nona McDonald's fingers brushed across the soft, worn calico of the old quilt on the top shelf of the cluttered closet, but just for a moment. A sudden, hard tug on her arm yanked her forward as though the quilt itself had grabbed her wrist and jerked with all its might. Too frightened to breathe, she felt herself hurtling headlong into a void where the linen closet had been just a moment earlier. The faint hum she had heard just before touching the quilt swelled to a roar in her ears. Within the roar, she heard hundreds of sounds, some recognizable, some not. She heard a car horn, glass breaking, gunfire, shouts and other noises that just blurred into an overwhelming, confusing din. Images of people and places raced past her eyes with dizzying speed as a crushing sensation in her chest forced all the air from her lungs until she thought she'd suffocate. Then, as suddenly as it had begun, it was over. But it wasn't over, because nothing around her made any sense anymore.

***

About three minutes before the world changed around her, Nona had pulled open the door of her grandmother's linen closet, shoved her long red curls into the back of her t-shirt to get them out of her way, and scanned the shelves for the sheets, pillowcases and quilt her grandmother had said were "right in front." It had been a year since she had last visited her grandparents' crazily-cluttered Durango, Colorado, house. Peering into the deep closet and taking stock of the overstuffed, floor-to-ceiling shelves, she realized it didn't look as looming as it used to. I *have* gotten taller, she thought, cringing with embarrassment at the memory of the scene her grandmother had created at the airport a few hours earlier.

Nona, now 13, had flown alone for the first time on this trip. She'd been feeling quite grown up from the moment she'd boarded the plane in Milwaukee until she stepped off the plane and into the little airport in Durango, Colorado. It was at that moment that her Grandma Ruth squealed, "You've gotten so ta-all," over the top of the crowd. A little over six feet tall, sporting a long mane of unruly gray curls and dressed in layers of mismatched, flowing clothing that looked a lot like costume shop castoffs, Nona's grandmother was always hard to miss. Dodging and weaving her way through a crowded airport while waving and yelling, she was impossible to ignore. When she had finally reached her granddaughter, she had flung her arms wide, stooped and enveloped the blushing girl and straightened up, lifting Nona in the process. Nona had rolled her eyes for effect, but had surrendered happily to the hug, her feet dangling limply about a foot from the floor.

"Don't touch the antique quilts on the upper shelves," her grandmother called from the guest room a couple of hours later, where she was busily collecting books, magazines and stray antique odds and ends from the dresser tops and bedside tables. "Take one of the newer ones on the middle shelves. The sheets are on the bottom shelf." The instructions were followed by the thudding of several books hitting the floor, a little muttering and the sounds of drawers being opened and closed.

Her grandparents, both college professors, lived in a huge, brick Victorian-era house in old Durango. The house was a constantly changing sea of books, magazines, antiques and hobby projects, peppered with countless boxes of inexplicable odds and ends. The wide hallway in which Nona stood was home to three tall Hoosier cabinets and two barrister bookcases. Each of the beautiful pieces of furniture was buried under, among other things, bolts of fabric, several pillow forms, a leather wig head, a few tattered footballs, a cookie tin full of sea shells, at least a dozen candlesticks, three antique telephones and a faded, smiling teddy bear.

"I know," Nona called toward the bedroom in answer to her grandmother's warning about the quilts, and turned back to the closet. With a mother, grandmother and several aunts who quilted, she had been a little girl when she learned the first rule of handling antique quilts: never touch the quilts with your bare hands, as skin can leave traces of oils on the quilts that will stain the fabric over time. Nona smiled seeing the white gloves, a sort of uniform for quilters handling antiques, hanging from a nail inside the closet's doorframe. Avoiding the older quilts on the uppers shelves, she began to reach for a brightly colored quilt on a shelf near her waist. She knew the fabric, a neon-colored collage of cat figures, couldn't possibly be an antique. But as she reached out for it, a bit of motion on the top shelf caught her eye. Turning her attention to the old quilts stored on the higher shelves, Nona realized the surface of a brown, off-white and green patchwork quilt was shimmering and moving ever so slightly. She gasped, took a step back and crinkled up her nose, certain there must be a mouse burrowing in the folds of the quilt. Watching the quilt for the little critter to appear, she realized quickly that there was no mouse. It was the quilt itself that was shifting and rippling like waves on a lake. She stretched up onto her tiptoes and leaned in to get a better look. Her brow wrinkled and her eyes squinted as she realized there was a humming sound coming from the quilt as well.

"Gram," she called to her still-muttering grandmother, "what's up with your quilts?" Nona couldn't take her eyes off the shimmering fabric and couldn't resist touching it, despite the ironclad rule. Her hand came up, without her consent, and she watched it move toward the age-softened fabric of the quilt. She noticed that the air seemed much warmer near the quilt than in the rest of the hallway and that the hum began to separate into several distant sounds. Nona heard a voice calling a name, something like Minnie or Lynnie. Frightened, yet unable to stop herself, she reached out toward the quilt, her fingers drawn to it like metal shavings to a magnet.

***

When the whirlwind of sounds, images and smells subsided, Nona blinked her eyes, repeatedly and vigorously, trying to make the sight before her disappear. The hallway and closet of Nona's grandparents' house were gone. In their place was a small, rough attic bedroom in what looked to be a log house. Nona was slumped on an uneven plank floor, beneath a small, open window that was covered by plain white curtains that were fluttering slightly in a gentle breeze. She took a deep, sniffling gulp of air, drawing in a lungful of very strange smells. Too frightened to move, she identified the smells as a tangy mix of wood smoke, coffee, biscuits, fried eggs and something very earthy. A horse nickered somewhere outside the window, explaining the non-food smells. Directly in front of Nona was an unmade, sagging double bed, with an old-fashioned, metal headboard and footboard that had been painted a shiny white. She gasped when she spotted the antique quilt she had just touched in her grandmother's closet. But it looked crisp and new where it lay tangled with the bed sheets. Her gasp was repeated behind her.

Terrified of what she would find, Nona cringed and turned slowly toward the sound and found a girl about her own age standing just a few feet away. She wore an ankle-length, white flannel nightgown and had her thick, brown hair woven into two braids that reached to her waist. Looking as though she might faint at any moment, the girl clamped her hand over her mouth and pressed her back into the corner of the room. Nona, who had had the wind knocked out of her in whatever it was that had landed her here, coughed and started to ask, "Where am … " But at that moment the girl and

3

then the entire room began to shimmer and grow dim. The roar returned and Nona covered her face in fear. She felt herself jolted, backwards this time, into the same rush of motion and sound she had been hurtled through a few minutes earlier. The sensations ended with a bang as her back slammed into something hard. She heard herself groan and felt herself slide to the floor. Then everything went dark.

"Oh dear, oh dear." Nona could feel her grandmother slapping her face. "Where did you go? HILDIE! I told her we should tell you. HILDIE! Oh, dear. Where and when did you go, child? HILDIE!"

The slapping and the shouts for her Aunt Hildie brought Nona to her senses. Before she could stop herself, she began crying for all she was worth. Her Grandma Ruth, who was also crying, helped her up off the floor, put an arm around her waist and steered her through the hallway and down the broad stairway to the den. Nona's knees felt like rubber and her head was still spinning as her grandmother settled her on the couch. Moving like the wind, her grandmother rushed back upstairs and returned with a red fleece bathrobe, telling Nona to put it on and promising to explain everything. She then hurried into the kitchen, where Nona heard her filling the hot water kettle and lighting the stove before digging in her mammoth handbag. Nona heard her hurry through the door and onto the back porch, accompanied by a soft beeping as she punched numbers into a cell phone.

Nona had no idea what had just happened, but it seemed to be an extension of the strange things that had been going on at home in the weeks before her parents had put her on the plane to Colorado. She felt suddenly queasy as she thought of the last few weeks. Something had been wrong. Her parents had been tense and distracted and she had felt somehow caught in the center of whatever the problem was. She had begun having trouble concentrating at school and had started having vivid, exhausting dreams that felt more real than her daily life. And then Nona had fainted, twice, on a field trip to the Milwaukee County Historical Society.

The field trip had been the breaking point, she thought, as she remembered that confusing day. She and her best friend, Alyssa, had been walking through the displays with the rest of their class when they stepped up to the velvet ropes surrounding an old-fashioned Model A car. Alyssa's voice, which had been droning on about cheerleading tryouts, had suddenly disappeared, replaced by one of Nona's startling dreams. She dreamt she was standing in the middle of a muddy city street with horses and buggies moving past her, along with shiny new versions of the car she had just been looking at and several of the old-time bicycles she had seen in pictures, with a front wheel as tall as Nona and a tiny wheel in the back. Men were shouting to her from the buggies, bicycles and cars, warning her to move out of the way, while on the side of the street, women called out to her with their arms outstretched. When she tried to turn away, she found herself sprawled on the marble floor of the Historical Society building, with her teacher frowning and bending over her.

A can of root beer and a little time spent sitting on a bench had made her feel better, at least until the class moved to the World War II "Rosie the Riveter" display. Nona had been reading the placard for a display of airplane parts made by women during the war when she began to hear the sounds of machinery and smell a strange, hot oil scent. Once again, she had slipped into one of her dreams, this time of a huge, noisy factory full of women working in jeans and denim shirts with bandanas covering their hair. She woke up on the floor looking up at her teacher again. Her mother arrived shortly after that to pick her up and had put her on the plane to Colorado the next morning, promising to follow with Nona's father as soon as possible. Her parents had promised to explain everything in Colorado and that things would be fine, but Nona wasn't so sure.

Having no idea what had happened in the closet, Nona didn't want to move lest it happen again. She sat still as a rock on the couch, trying to run her mind back over the day, from getting up extra early in order to catch her flight, to Grandpa Fred joining them at the restaurant in Durango for lunch, to working on clearing out the guest room with her grandmother. But her mind kept drifting further back, recalling the dreams she had been having back in Milwaukee. She thought that the voice she had heard in the closet, calling for someone named Minnie or Lynnie, was familiar to her. She had heard it before. She had heard it, she realized, in the dreams that she had been having at home – the dreams that seemed to be part of whatever had just happened to her. The name, she suddenly knew, was Winnie.

Nona became aware of her grandmother on the porch speaking into the phone in a hushed tone. It didn't strike her as particularly odd, as both of her grandparents were prone to rather strange behavior in the first place. They both taught history and archeology at Fort Lewis College in Durango and spent a lot of time traveling to archeological digs and libraries around the world. Their travels were the reason she almost never counted on catching them at home when she called. They were also both just a little flaky, or as Nona's father put it, "absent-minded professors." Keeping track of things like keys, cell phones and the day of the week seemed impossible for both of them. Yet, either one of them could, and often would, tell you everything there was to know about the Anasazi civilization that once thrived across the southwest, that the modern zipper was designed in 1913 and that the transistor radio appeared in 1954. They both had a gift for talking about history, both recent and distant, as though it had happened just a few days ago and that they had been there to see it. They filled their stories and explanations with such details and descriptions that they brought it all to life for the listener.

Sitting on the couch, Nona surveyed the clutter that surrounded her. Like the guest bedroom, the living and dining rooms and the rest of the house, her grandparents' den was awash in a sea of books, academic journals and an unrelated collection of antiques and odds and ends. Grandpa Fred had taken up the trombone in recent years and had dedicated one end of the den to practice space. His horn, chair and music stand stood there like sentries awaiting his return, surrounded, unaccountably, by a cast iron sausage press, a crockery butter churn, several World War I artillery shells and a rusted egg basket filled to the brim with old, wooden thread spindles. The corner of the living room that Nona could see from her seat on the couch in the den was filled by her grandmother's oversized quilting frame, which was clearly too big to fit in her sewing room, or any other room in the house. The quilt currently in progress was covered with a faded, blue bed sheet, on top of which lay Baxter, their lazy gray and white cat. Baxter had lifted his head to stare at Nona as her grandmother had helped her to the couch, but had apparently decided his nap was more interesting than whatever the humans were up to. Nona had a fleeting moment of curiosity about Baxter, remembering that it seemed to her as though the same cat was in photos of her grandparents' house going back to her mother's childhood. She was distracted from her thoughts when she heard the hot water kettle begin to whistle on the stove. She stood up to turn off the flame under it, but a wave of dizziness sent her slumping back to the couch.

Grandma Ruth, hurrying in from the porch to tend to the kettle, saw her drop to the couch and called out, "You're fine now, just sit tight. We'll have tea in two shakes." She then rushed into the kitchen, turned off the flame under the kettle and began clanking tea mugs and spoons.

"I know you're frightened," Grandma Ruth said, bringing in a tray that held a steaming pot of what smelled like orange tea, along with two big mugs painted with Christmas greetings and a small plate of cookies. "I know I was when it happened to me. Your Aunt Hildie was a wreck when she Traveled for the first time and your Aunt Anna was terrified for weeks. It's just plain upsetting at first. But this is really a gift. It's something rare and wonderful. I know you'll come to appreciate it."

Nona had no idea why her grandmother was going on about her traveling to Durango being a rare and wonderful gift. She had been spending part of her summers with her grandparents since she was a little girl. Nothing rare there. Traveling to Durango wasn't what had Nona upset, she thought a little peevishly. It was what had happened after she arrived.

She allowed herself to be distracted by the Scottish shortbread cookies, her favorites, which her grandmother had included on the tray. She shoveled an entire cookie into her mouth, knowing full well that it was rude, but she couldn't help herself. In the next instant the room was filled with a loud hum, followed by a sudden pop and a nearly blinding flash of blue light that somehow produced her Aunt Hildie. Nona's mouth fell open and cookie shards tumbled unheeded onto the fleece robe.

Elaine Schmidt

CHAPTER 2

"Oh for heaven's sake, Hildie. Couldn't you just once knock and make a polite entrance?" Grandma Ruth's skin had gone a rather startling shade of red as she read Hildie the riot act. "This poor girl has been scared witless by her first Visit and then you come blasting into the room like Fourth of July fireworks. I should think you of all people might be a little more considerate. It's just a good thing she didn't have a mug of tea in her hand yet. She might have scalded herself."

"You're right, Mom. I'm sorry," Hildie said, using as contrite a tone as Nona had ever heard from her. "I've been keeping an eye on her for months now, so I knew she was going to Travel soon. I just couldn't be sure when it would happen."

Aunt Hildie set a large, tattered carpet bag in the corner, smoothed the black skirt that reached to the top of her ankle-high, lace-up boots, tugged the bottom of the very old-fashioned-looking, waist-length, fitted, black jacket she was wearing and tidied the ornate twist that held her long, brown hair against the back of her head.

Nona looked back and forth between the two women, who had begun speaking as though she weren't in the room. Curious, frightened and coughing from the cookie crumbs she had just inhaled, Nona was also a little irritated by the fact that no one was talking to her. She practically shouted as she asked, "What are you talking about?"

"Indoor voice, dear," Grandma Ruth said, frowning at Nona. "No need to shout." She turned to Hildie and said, "I've told Lois."

"You talked to Mom?" Nona asked, but the two women either didn't hear her or ignored her, lost in their own conversation.

"Really Mother, I think she has a right to shout or whisper or whatever else she may feel like doing at this point. Her life, after all, has changed in ways she could never have anticipated," Hildie said, sounding a bit irked herself.

Aunt Hildie, Nona's mother's older sister, was regarded throughout the family as something of a free spirit. She was also a major mystery in Nona's life. Although she had asked many times what her Aunt Hildie did for a living and where she lived, the answers were always vague and never quite the same. As a result, Nona didn't know much of anything about her aunt, except that she was an awful lot of fun and the rest of the family paled beside her. She had a way of showing up at the last minute for family events, and disappearing again just as suddenly. Nona had concocted several dramatic stories in her mind to explain her unconventional aunt, but in her heart she knew none of them were true. Somehow she knew for the first time that the truth was going to be wilder than anything she had imagined.

Nona stood up and paced back and forth as her grandmother and aunt continued discussing her situation. They spoke about how she must be feeling and what they should do next. Irritated, Nona turned sharply to face the two of them, throwing herself just a little off balance in the process. As she took a step backwards to brace herself, Nona felt her leg hit the footed, cast iron pot that always sat beside the fireplace. She turned to look at it, expecting to see it full of Baxter's cat toys, as usual, but instead felt the same tug she had felt before Winnie's quilt pulled her into the past.

"No," she shouted, oblivious to the fact that Aunt Hildie and her grandmother had both reached out to grab her arms. They nearly reached her, but not quite, before she disappeared.

Nona felt the blur of sounds, smells and images she recognized from her quilt encounter. It ended with an unceremonious bang as the cast iron pot fell over, spilling what looked like a pile of well-worn work gloves onto a battered wooden floor. Nona plopped to the floor herself a moment later.

"A porch," she muttered, stunned by having been rocketed to someplace strange again, but keenly aware that she wasn't as frightened as she had been the first time it happened. The porch was bathed in warm sunlight, she noticed, looking around. She gasped, realizing that the cabinet beside which she had landed was a newer-looking version of the one that had stood in her grandmother's kitchen as long as she could remember. She put her hand on the cabinet and began pulling herself to her feet when a door at the end of the porch swung open and a woman who looked like an older, plumper version of her grandmother stepped through and gasped at the sight of the girl on her porch. Nona plopped back down onto the porch floor in shock.

"Oh dear," the woman said in a worried voice. She gave Nona a good, long stare before saying, "You don't belong here, do you?"

"No ... I ... well," Nona had no idea what to say. The woman's resemblance to her grandmother stopped at the neck, Nona thought, taking in the woman's simple, mid-calf-length cotton dress, lace-up leather shoes and rumpled apron. Although she had hair the same color as Nona's grandmother, it was all pinned up in an elaborate bun at the back of her head. But it wasn't the resemblance to her grandmother that had Nona tongue-tied. She had no clue how to explain how and why she was on the woman's porch.

"Don't worry dear, I'm sure Hildie will be along for you in a moment. Nona, isn't it?" She took a few brisk steps to where Nona was sitting on the floor and extended a hand to help her up.

"Hildie?" Nona asked as the woman led her through the door into a tidy kitchen that looked like a museum exhibit on household life in the early-20th century. A big, yellow bowl sat on the counter. Nona could see a thick, doughy blob of some sort in the bowl, with the wooden handle of what Nona guessed was a spoon poking up out of it. The air in the room was thick with aromas of cinnamon and baking apples.

"Don't worry, I know your Aunt Hildie quite well. It's pie day," the woman said in a matter of fact tone. "Have a seat and help yourself to an apple, if you like."

"Who are you?" Nona blurted, still standing stock still in the middle of the kitchen. She knew it sounded rude, but didn't particularly care at the moment.

"Oh, of course. I'm sorry," the woman said, wiping her hands on her apron and smoothing a few stray hairs back in places. "My name is Helen and I guess I must be your great-great aunt. Perhaps you should just call me Aunt Helen."

As Aunt Helen was speaking, Nona heard a faint humming sound in the distance. It grew louder and louder until Nona could barely hear her great-great aunt. The woman seemed completely unaware of the roar until a flash of blue light and a loud pop announced Aunt Hildie's arrival.

"Oh dear," Aunt Helen said, clearly startled. "That's quite an arrival, young lady."

"Sorry, Aunt Helen, I didn't mean to startle you." Hildie sounded a bit breathless. "I just wanted to get to Nona as quickly as I could. She sort of disappeared on us."

The two spoke for a moment, Hildie explaining what had just happened and Aunt Helen taking it in and nodding knowingly. Nona frowned, irritated all over again by people talking about her like she wasn't in the room. She decided the apple Aunt Helen had offered sounded like a good idea and took one from the basket on the end of the counter. Turning to look for a place to sit, she spotted a well-worn wooden stool near the door to the porch and sat.

The next thing Nona was aware of was a blur of the two women shouting something along the lines of "No, not there," and the increasingly familiar rush of images flying by. The sensation reminded her of seeing a film sped up until images and sounds blurred into a constant stream of nonsense.

This time the sensation stopped only to be replaced by a slow, jerky, rocking motion. She was in a stiflingly hot, dusty little space, sitting on what felt like a pile of lumber. A bizarre combination of the sounds of creaking wood, horse hooves hitting dirt, fabric flapping in the wind and a man's voice added to her disorientation.

Looking around, she sorted out that she must be in a covered wagon, sitting on top of a mountain of goods that some family was carting with them, when a blue glow filled the air around her and Aunt Hildie's head appeared in front of her.

"Take my hand," Hildie whispered, looking around at the surrounding herself. Her hand appeared out of nowhere, reaching toward Nona.

Nona dropped the apple she had forgotten she was holding, reached up and took Hildie's hand gratefully. Once again she felt the familiar tug and then the swirling sensations of moving through time. The sensations began to slow and images became more distinct for a few moments, before she and Hildie landed neatly on their feet in front of her grandmother's couch.

Hildie began to tell Grandma Ruth about Nona's most recent leaps through time, punctuated by clucks and comments from the older woman. Just as Nona thought she might burst if someone didn't start talking to her, Aunt Hildie turned to her and said, "We have a lot to explain to you. I think it's best to start with a few questions."

Nona took a deep breath to start asking the hundred or so questions flying around in her mind at the moment, but Aunt Hildie beat her to it.

"Have you had dreams recently that were so real that you seemed to experience things like smells and tastes?"

Nona, feeling as though her mind was being read, nodded silently.

"How about dreams where you're doing something like walking in the rain and then you wake up with wet hair?"

Nona nodded again, remembering the night before her birthday when she dreamt that she had fallen into a shallow river and woke up dripping wet. The next morning she found a big bruise on her knee, just where it hit a rock as she fell into the river in her dream. She tried to tell her mother about the dreams, but she had just said it was an overactive imagination and that if Nona ignored these dreams they would go away. But her mother had begun looking worried and hovering over everything Nona did.

"Those dreams weren't actually dreams," Hildie said deliberately, watching her niece as though measuring Nona's response to her words. Grandma Ruth looked at her daughter and nodded encouragingly. "They were little Visits to other places and times," Hildie said.

Nona tried to process what that might mean, unaware of the confusion registering on her face.

"You're what's known as a Traveler," Aunt Hildie said, her eyes glued to Nona's face. "I'm a Traveler … "

"Me too," Grandma Ruth interrupted, "and your folks and … "

"Travelers are people who can slip around in time," Aunt Hildie said, interrupting her mother with a stern look. "It's usually accidental at first and pretty unnerving, like what happened to you upstairs a little while ago. But with some study and practice, you'll learn to control it and enjoy it." She shot another stern glance at Grandma Ruth, who was just inhaling as though she wanted to add something.

"For the moment though, you'll have to be very careful," Aunt Hildie continued. "Clearly objects from the past have a strong pull for you, so you'll want to avoid touching your skin to anything that could trigger Travel until you know how to handle it. There are rules to be learned too. The Commission doesn't take kindly to having to tidy up temporal messes. It seems as though your little Visit was triggered by touching Winnie's quilt."

Aunt Hildie looked around the room, with its collection of antiques from various eras and artifacts from archeological digs.

"Good grief, Mom, this place is a veritable mine field of accidental Travel possibilities."

Gram glanced around the room, a look of dismay coming over her face, before hurrying off to the kitchen and returning a moment later, waving the bright pink, lace-trimmed rubber gloves that usually resided draped on the edge of a plastic bucket beneath the kitchen sink. "For the moment, keep these gloves on your hands at all times. That way you can't touch something you shouldn't and pop off to the past."

Nona pulled on the floppy gloves that smelled vaguely of scouring powder. Her grandmother retrieved a ball of yarn from the clutter on the end table beside the couch and bit off a couple of lengths, tying them around Nona's wrists to hold the gloves in place. Looking around the room, Nona shuddered, understanding for the first time that the bits of ancient Native American pottery, apothecary bottles and antique dolls were not just part of the fascinating clutter of her grandparents' home – they were threatening objects that could grab her and fling her instantly into some far-off corner of the past.

"Do people ever not come back?" Nona asked, feeling her stomach knot up at the thought. The notion of plopping into another time and place with no way to get home made her feel more alone than she had ever imagined a person could feel.

After a long, tense pause and several glances shared with Aunt Hildie, Grandma Ruth said, "It can happen. I had … have … a sister, Ruda. We were on a castle tour in England during the summer before I went into the

6th grade and she went into the 8th. There was a beautiful suit of armor, chain mail and all, in a hallway. The docent told us we could touch the chain mail if we wanted to, so Ruda did. Just as her hand touched the suit, there was a terrible bang and a flash of light. The suit of armor flew backwards, smashing into the wall a few yards away with a terrible racket and Ruda was gone." Large tears spilled down her tanned cheeks.

"What happened to her?" Nona felt like a little kid waiting for the end of a sad fairy tale.

"We don't know," Grandma Ruth said, shaking her head. "My mother tried to find her, so did her sisters and their mother and the Commission. But they never could. I looked too, for years, and Hildie is working on it to this day."

"So everybody in the family does this traveling thing?" Nona's world was getting less familiar by the minute. "Even my mom and dad? And Grandpa?"

Her aunt and grandmother exchanged glances again before Aunt Hildie said, "Yes, nearly everyone in our family Travels at some point in their lives. Since it puts us in rather odd situations, most of the family has married Travelers too. As a result, our family's Travel abilities seem to grow with each generation."

"Nona dear, your name means The Ninth, did you know that?" her grandmother asked gently, patting Nona's shoulder.

Nona shook her head. She had always thought her name was odd, but its oddness paled in contrast to the other oddness in her family, so it had never occurred to her to ask about it.

"We knew when you were born that you would be a powerful Traveler. You are the ninth generation of Travelers in both our family and your father's family. It's something to be very proud of."

Nona didn't feel proud. Instead, she felt as though she had never known her own family at all. The more Nona thought about what had happened and what it meant, the more questions she found to ask and the more tired she became.

The ringing of her grandmother's cell phone jarred her back to the present. Her grandmother answered it, saying something about "upset, of course," before telling Nona it was her mother and handing her the phone.

"Nona?" her mother's voice sounded tense and worried. "Dad's right here. We're on speaker. Are you alright?"

Nona assured them that she was fine, although she was aware she sounded less than convincing. She had so many questions that she wanted to ask her parents that she had no idea where to start.

"I'm sure you have a mountain of questions, lass," her father said, the lilt of his Scottish accent and deliberately calm tone reassuring Nona as much through the phone as a hug would have. "We will be there as soon as we can. Then we'll have a good, long chat about all of this."

"We're leaving in just a little while," her mother said, sounding a little breathless at the thought. "It's a 21-hour drive, so we'll be there tomorrow evening. We'll have our cell phone on as we drive, so just call us if you want to talk."

"I'm glad you're coming," Nona said, sniffling a little as the smell of the rubber gloves made her nose itch. Actually, she was irritated that even with everything that had just happened, her father wouldn't fly. Whenever the topic came up he would carry on about "those great beasts," meaning airplanes, having no business in the sky. He would invariably end up muttering about daft people "hurtling through the clouds" and shaking his head vehemently. He was not going to fly, she knew, not even now. They spoke for a few more minutes, her parents reassuring her that she would be fine until they arrived, before her mother said they had a lot to do before they started driving.

After Nona got off the phone, the tiredness came flooding back. Aunt Hildie and Grandma Ruth told her a nap would make her feel better, promising that they would take turns sitting beside her as she snoozed. Nona knew it was worry about her popping off to the past, not concern over her getting some much-needed sleep, that had them effectively standing guard over her. Needing someone to watch over her while she slept made Nona even more nervous than she had been about everything she had learned. But worried as she was, she could barely keep her eyes open. She wanted to talk to her parents too, but felt her eyes closing and knew she had to sleep before she did anything else. Nona struggled with pajamas, the rubber gloves complicating every move. She eventually tossed them aside, tumbled into bed in her clothes and fell asleep in minutes – a sleep full of terrifyingly real dreams.

Elaine Schmidt

CHAPTER 3

Nona opened her eyes the next morning and lay perfectly still for a moment, her heart racing. She had been so exhausted and slept so deeply that it took a few minutes to remember that she was at her grandparents' house. It took a little longer to remember what had happened the day before. Neither Aunt Hildie nor Grandma Ruth was in the room when Nona looked around, but Grandpa Fred was. The tall, salt-and-pepper-haired man looked like he had folded himself in two to get into the small, Victorian armchair beside the bed. He wore a comfortably rumpled plaid shirt and soft, faded jeans with scuffed, loose-fitting loafers and no socks, giving him a relaxed, happy-to-be-at-home look. His reading glasses were perched low on his nose and he had a pencil tucked behind each ear. He was taking notes with a third pencil, writing on a legal pad that was perched on the cluttered table between the bed and the chair.

"Morning, Sweetie," he said, his bright blue eyes sparkling warmly over the top of his glasses and a gentle smile spreading across his tanned, deeply-lined face. "I hear you had quite an afternoon after we parted company yesterday."

"Yesterday? What time is it?" Nona was confused. She couldn't have slept all evening and then all night, could she? She reached up to rub her eyes and was startled by the big, pink, rubber gloves tied in place on her hands.

"It's about 9:30," he said, not bothering to look at his watch. Grandpa Fred had what he called an "internal chronometer." No matter when you asked him, no matter what he was doing, he could always tell you what time it was, to within a couple of minutes. He joked that it was a good thing he always knew the time since Grandma Ruth never had a clue what time it was. He was right, Nona thought.

"It's not unusual for Travelers to be completely exhausted by their experiences, especially their first ones," he said. "I remember my first Visit. I think I was gone for about five minutes and then slept for about 10 hours. But you get used to it and it gets easier."

"How come I never knew any of this about our family?" Nona asked, snuggling down under the cat-themed quilt and settling in for a chat. She remembered her grandmother pulling an old quilt off the bed the night before and replacing it with the cat quilt, explaining that she didn't want Nona popping off to the past in her sleep.

"Well, it's not the easiest thing to explain to someone who doesn't Travel, let alone to a child," he said, looking her straight in the eye. Grandpa Fred always talked to children the same way he talked to adults. He was direct, honest and didn't dumb down what he said just because his audience was young. "There was also the danger of having you mention it to someone outside the family. Until you begin to Travel yourself, you really don't understand how sensitive the topic can be."

"I'm not sure I know what you mean."

"No, I suppose not." He took off his glasses and put them on top of his head, which made Nona smile. He did this so often with his glasses that most of the time he didn't even realize he had done it. In a little while, when he was ready to read again, he would look around the table, check his shirt pocket and then start looking around the rest of the house for his glasses. Eventually he would remember where they were, or someone would point them out to him. Sometimes he would get a second pair and spend several hours with one pair on top of his head while reading through another pair.

"Imagine," he continued, "how crazy it would make our family sound if you started talking to people about any one of us going back in time. Or if you told a story about your Grandpa seeing the Civil War battle of Antetum or witnessing the landing of the Mayflower. Or what about the fact that your Dad was born in 1722? What if that slipped out? Travelers have to be very careful about the Chrono-Bound, you know. They just don't do well with this sort of information."

"What do you mean my dad was born in 1722?" Nona blurted. The explanations she had gotten from her aunt and grandmother the day before had raised more questions than they had answered, but her grandfather's last statement raised one question too many. The feeling of confusion she had awoken with had been ebbing as they spoke, but that statement brought it back in full force.

"Oh, I forgot. Your parents haven't had a chance to sit down and talk to you since this happened, have they?" Grandpa Fred looked genuinely sorry. "Your father was born in 1722. He and your mother met while they were both Traveling. They fell in love – you know it's quite common for Travelers to marry other Travelers. No one understands the life of a Traveler other than another Traveler. But when you fall in love with someone from another time, even another Traveler, you run the risk of heartbreak. By and large, you can't just take a contemporary person and successfully plop them in the past or vice versa – you can't just pull someone out of the past and let their time play out without them. There is the Time Continuum to think about."

"The what?"

"The Time Continuum." Grandpa swiped his big hand across his face as though clearing away any stray thoughts that might be cluttering his mind. He always did this before telling a story or, according to his students, before he delivered a class lecture or explanation.

"Let's use your mom as an example. Let's say she went back in time as a young woman and fell in love with another Traveler who lived in the 1700s, which of course is just what she did. But let's say that according to history he was to fight at the Battle of Culloden, survive it and go on to write the definitive history of the battle. Let's go a little further forward and say that he was supposed to marry and raise five children. You still with me?"

"Sort of. Keep going." Nona had some pretty big questions, but she knew her grandfather well enough to trust that he would explain away most of them before long.

"There is a group of Travelers whose job it is to keep the Timeline in check. They're called Monitors. Mature Travelers leave what are called Signatures, although it seems to me they might as well be called trails. Some, though not very many, Travelers can sense and follow through time. Essentially these Signatures follow the Traveler, marking where they started and where they went. The Monitors get their jobs in part because they have the ability to sense and follow the Signatures. As soon as a Signature appears in an era, they begin monitoring the Timeline to check for alterations." He paused, taking a long look at Nona.

"Go on," she said, trying to wrap her mind around all of this information.

"The Monitors have access to a great library of history called the Master Chronoscript. It's essentially the history of the world as it has occurred up to the present moment."

"Oh, without any Travelers?" Nona thought she understood.

"Not exactly. Travelers have always existed and have had a hand in many world events. Their Travels and the impacts they have made on the world are recorded in the Chronoscript. Your father's future was not what I described to you. He was one of the first killed in a terrible battle at a place in Scotland known as Culloden Moor, and was buried there in a mass grave with other men of the McDonald clan."

The thought of her father dead and buried almost three centuries ago was hard to take. Nona felt her throat tighten up the way it always did before she started to cry. She swallowed hard.

"The Monitors can only look back, they can't look forward, just as we, well at least the vast majority of us, can't Travel forward. They knew that your mother could bring him to her own time to live out his life in our time and that it would not have an impact on the Time Continuum as they knew it. So they gave your parents permission to try and make the leap to your mother's time. There was no guarantee that it would work, and some danger. They had to rely on your mother's abilities, since your father could Travel back but not forward in time. They decided to try it and, as you can already guess, it went swimmingly."

"So Dad was born in 1722 in Scotland." It wasn't a question. It was more of an amazed statement. A lot of things fell into place for Nona as she thought about this fact. "That's why I've never met anyone from his side of my family - they all lived 300 years ago. That's why his Scottish accent is so different from Mrs. Fraser, the Scottish lady who runs the cafeteria at my school." She rubbed a hand over her face, in a junior version of her grandfather's gesture that neither of them recognized at the moment.

"Yes, and it's also why he won't fly and why he works making handmade furniture that your mother sells in her shop. He has no birth certificate in this time. He is 'off the grid' as the kids say. He can't get a Social Security number and therefore can't get a job or a passport," her grandfather said, watching her face as he spoke.

Nona was doing the mental math one does when adding new facts to what one already knows about a situation. Her father's habit of catching himself and stopping every time he had cause to mention his parents and siblings made sense for the first time. His fascination with Scottish history, his occupation and even his speech pattern, which was filled with terms no one else used, all fell into place for her. His refusal to get on an airplane and the fact that she had only seen him drive the car once were also starting to make some sense. She thought about her father driving on the day she fell and cut her chin. Her father had driven her to the hospital for stitches, the car lurching and weaving through the streets as he shouted at drivers, bikers and pedestrians all the way there. He refused to drive back home, waiting for Nona's mother to arrive so she could do the driving.

"Oh good, you're up," her grandmother chirped, interrupting Nona's thoughts as she sailed into the room with a cup of coffee for Grandpa Fred. "You'd better get a move on. We have a big day ahead of us. Your parents will be here shortly and we have a lot of work to do. Keep those gloves on. There are slippers beside the bed for you. Put them on and keep them on for now. We don't need you stepping on one of the old Turkish rugs and popping out on us. I'm working on something that should solve the problem in short order." She hurried to the windows, and pulled up the shades to let in the blazing mountain sunlight before heading for the kitchen at her usual clip.

Nona made her way into the kitchen more slowly, shuffling her feet carefully to keep her grandmother's slippers on her feet. They were a few sizes too big to make walking comfortable, but she quickly decided walking slowly was preferable to plopping into some centuries-old harem. She was also moving slowly to try and sort through the odd sounds she was hearing. The coat rack at the end of the hall seemed to be producing the sound of a child crying, the sound of a thunderstorm was wafting from the muddy hiking boots near the front door, and so on.

The kitchen table was cluttered with what looked like the remains of a grade-school art project. Several flowers, each missing quite a few leaves and petals, a strip of suede, bits of leather, scissors, a pin cushion stuck full of needles and pins, and an open sewing box bursting with odds and ends were all strewn around the table. The quilt that had started everything the day before was draped on the back of one of the chairs at the table. Nona took a step back, suddenly afraid of the quilt and where it might send her. Her grandmother appeared from the living room tying a last knot on something in her hand.

"Let's see if we can't lose those gloves," she said, wrinkling her nose at the site of Nona's hands. "I made you a homing pouch. This should keep you anchored in the present until you learn to control your Travel abilities." She held out a small fabric pouch attached to a thin strip of leather.

"What is it? Nona asked, reaching out a gloved hand to touch it. Rethinking, she pulled her gloved hand back and looked closely at the pouch without touching it instead. She wanted breakfast, not another traumatic trip to who knows when.

"It's a little homing pouch I made this morning. I filled it with petals from flowers that I picked from the garden this morning and a few bits of fabrics that I stitched together into a tiny, tiny quilt block. All of these things have a strong connection with this morning. The flower petals didn't exist until they opened up this morning. Same with the quilt square, since I just made it a little while ago. Even the pouch itself was made this morning."

"This will keep me from traveling?" Nona asked hopefully and a bit dubiously.

"It should do the trick to keep you in one place and time as you learn to control your abilities – at least as long as it's touching your skin," her grandmother said. She strung the leather strip around Nona's neck and decided on a good length for it. She snipped off the extra and pulled a threaded needle from the front of her shirt. She knotted the thread, stitched the loose end of the leather strip to the pouch to make a necklace of it for Nona, and then tied off the thread to hold it in place.

"There," she said, mumbling as she bit off the remaining thread from the strap. She stuck the needle in the pincushion on the table and slipped the loop over Nona's head. "Tuck that inside your shirt so it rests against your skin and, for heaven's sake, leave it there."

Nona followed her grandmother's instructions. She felt the pouch make contact with her skin and gasped. The moment the pouch had touched her chest the room had brightened around her and the sounds emanating from nearly every object around her dropped to a dull murmur.

"What just happened, Sweetie?" her grandmother asked.

Nona hesitated for a moment, looking around at the kitchen before answering. "I feel more normal," she responded, surprised to realize that she hadn't felt quite right until that moment.

"Explain," her grandmother said, sounding just a little impatient.

"I didn't notice it until it changed, I guess," Nona said, looking around the room one more time. "But it was almost as though things were dim in here, as though the shades were down and there wasn't enough light to see everything clearly. And it sounded sort of like the television and the radio and maybe the stereo were all on at once until I put this on. The second it touched my skin it was like the lights came on and all the noise got much quieter."

"Not a moment too soon then," her grandmother pointed at the gloves. "Tell me exactly what you saw yesterday when you Traveled. In just a minute we'll get rid of those."

Nona described the room, the girl, the quilt and all the smells and sounds of the overwhelming experience.

"I thought so," her grandmother said with a triumphant tone in her voice. "When you Traveled yesterday you went to my Great-Great Aunt Winnie Longenecker's bedroom in 1898. She made that quilt for her hope chest, but wanted to use it for a few nights before she packed it away. The fact that it was on her bed means that it had to be one of just a couple of possible days in that particular spring."

The year, 1898, made Nona feel a little woozy and somehow sad. It was the same deep-down sadness she had felt the first time she went to sleep-away camp in the third grade. Her mother told her then that it was just old-fashioned homesickness that made her feel that way. She had said that remembering that she would be coming home soon would make it go away, and she had been right. But 1898 – Nona couldn't help wondering what would happen if she couldn't get home from another century. It would take more than a hundred years to catch up with the present and her family. Tears started to well up as she thought about never seeing her mom and dad or grandparents again.

"Oh dear," her grandmother saw her tears and hurried to tuck Nona's unruly, sleep-tousled hair behind her ears and then rested a comforting hand on her shoulder. "You wouldn't have been stuck there, at least not for long. We would have come for you. But this pouch takes away the chance of going somewhere you don't want to go and will help you get back to this morning if you're Traveling. Eventually, as you learn how to Travel safely, you'll only carry one of these for emergencies, but for now you will wear it at all times. You will wear it under your clothing and your jammies, touching your skin. You may take it off to shower, but you must keep it within reach to grab if you feel any signs of Traveling. You must put it on the moment you turn off the water."

Nona nodded and sniffled, feeling herself calm down. She had no intention of breaking these new rules and she knew that there was no one in the world who would rush to help her like her own family.

"Okay, let's put it to the test. Take off the gloves," her grandmother untied the yarn holding the gloves in place and Nona pulled them off slowly. "I want you to put your hand on Winnie's quilt. Don't worry, if you Travel, you will almost undoubtedly go to Winnie's room again. I'll know when and where you're headed and I'll be right behind you to fetch you back. But I don't think we'll need to worry about that."

Enjoying the cool, free feeling of having the gloves gone, Nona moved her right hand slowly and tentatively toward the quilt. As her hand got close to the fabric, she heard a faint hum – much fainter than the roar she had heard the day before. The room around her dimmed slightly and she caught a faint whiff of wood smoke and barnyard smells. She heard what sounded like someone chopping wood in the far distance. Nona felt a slight pull toward the quilt, more of an invitation than the sharp, inescapable tug that yanked her back in time the day before. She pulled her hand back, slowly, and felt herself return completely to her grandmother's kitchen and her grandmother's intent stare.

"So?" Her grandmother looked like someone who had just won a bet.

"I could hear and smell things from Winnie's farm, but really faintly this time," Nona said. "The kitchen got sort of dark, like the lights dimmed a little bit. I could feel a little pull to the quilt, but nothing like yesterday."

"Well then, we're in business," her grandmother began clearing the project mess from the table, transferring it all to an already cluttered end table, and assigned Nona and her grandfather breakfast-making tasks. They were just sitting down to steaming bowls of oatmeal topped with fresh strawberries when Nona heard a hum. Noticing that it was getting louder, she looked up and waited for the arrival she knew was about to occur. Within a few seconds, Aunt Hildie arrived with a loud pop and flash of blue light.

Elaine Schmidt

CHAPTER 4

"Just in time for breakfast," Hildie chimed, pulling off a weathered denim jacket that was painted with flowers and peace symbols. She was wearing a yellowed, tie-dyed t-shirt and tattered jeans. She had a faded, red bandana on her head and a dirty, green backpack slung over one shoulder.

"How was the concert?" Nona's grandfather asked, kissing his daughter on the cheek and setting another place at the table.

"Concert?" Nona asked, the oatmeal in her mouth getting in the way of the word. She realized it would take a while to get used to people popping in like stray thoughts.

"I smell coffee," Hildie said with a hungry look toward the kitchen. "Woodstock, sweetheart. I was at the most famous concert in the history of rock and roll."

"I've heard of that," Nona said, frowning as she tried to remember what she had read about it. "It was on a farm, right? Sometime in the '60s?"

"Bingo! It happened in 1969, on Max Yasgur's farm in Bethel, New York. Some people see it as the greatest moment of an entire generation. Whether it was or wasn't, it was something completely unique and spontaneous that no one has ever been able to recreate. There were about 500,000 people there, but today, there are two or three times that number who claim to have been there."

"So, how was it?" Nona asked.

"Loud, muddy and wonderful," she said to Nona. Turning to her mother, she said, "What were you thinking with that hair?"

"*You* were there?" Nona wheeled around to face her grandmother, who was making some extra oatmeal for Hildie. Nona had a hard time envisioning her grandmother as a hippie.

"I was, and so was your grandfather. In fact, that's where he proposed to me," she said, with a note of pride in her voice. "We had a great time with the counterculture crowd that weekend, but it made us realize that we were both pretty traditional at heart. At least about our personal lives. And for your information," she said sternly, facing Hildie, "sleeping with your hair in dozens of tiny braids and then brushing it out in the morning to create that mass of tiny waves was considered very chic back in the day. Your big-hair days in the 80s, and for that matter the present generation's fascination with tattoos, are no better than fads of an era. At least yours and mine could be combed or cut."

"I'll take you there when you're old enough," Hildie said with a conspiratorial wink to Nona. "They spent the last day of the festival under a stand of trees way in the back of the crowd and off to the right of the stage. You've got to see the hair in person to believe it."

"Enough!" Grandpa Fred barked, with a grin that made it clear he had been enjoying the banter. "Eat up and don't dawdle. We have a lot to get done this morning, to say nothing of the afternoon's schedule. And it looks to me as though there's some costuming to be done as well." He gave pointed looks to Hildie in her denim and Nona in the rumpled clothing she had been wearing since the previous day. He explained that Nona's parents would be arriving any minute and the whole lot of them were going to help Nona get her Travel "sea legs," as he put it. Nona returned to her breakfast, but barely tasted it as she realized that she couldn't even imagine what the coming day might hold for her.

By the time Nona had helped clear the table and had taken a shower, being careful to keep her homing pouch nearby at all times, her grandmother had assembled several dozen odd items on a large tray, which she had set on the kitchen table. At first glance, Nona could recognize a silver serving ladle, a tiny comb, a gold pocket watch on a heavy gold chain, a small hook with an ornate, pearl handle, and a fragile-looking glass Christmas ornament. The rest of the items were a complete mystery.

"What's all of this?" Nona asked, but before her grandmother could answer, she heard the hum of an incoming Traveler. She tilted her head, thinking it sounded louder and somehow more labored than the hum Aunt Hildie made just before she arrived. She followed the sound to the dining room as the hum turned to an all-out whooshing sound. She arrived in the dining room just in time to see her parents appear with a pair of almost simultaneous, soft pops.

They were pressed close together with her mother holding tightly to her father's arm. They both staggered for a moment, as though they might topple over. Nona's dad grinned at her and disentangled himself from her mother's grip to reach out for his daughter. Her mother, looking winded and disconcerted, gave Nona a worried once over before joining in a long, family hug.

As they finally let go of one another, her grandparents and aunt crowded into the dining room, each shouting some version of "Hugh! Lois! You're here!" Then all of the adults began to talk at once. Nona used the moments of confusion to take a good look at her parents, feeling as though she had just met them for the first time. Her father's red, curly hair, clearly the origin of her own mane, was wildly wind blown. Although his broad, solid shoulders and steady hands hadn't changed since she had seen him yesterday at the airport, they suddenly seemed to her to be carved from something rare. Her mother used three quick movements to straighten her collar, pat her shoulder-length, brown hair into place and rescue her glasses from a precarious position on the tip of her nose. Thinking of them meeting in the 1700s took Nona's breath away.

"You Traveled?" Hildie asked, with a worried look on her face.

"I know, I know," Nona's mother said quickly, holding up her hands as though fending off an argument. "I know we're not allowed to Travel anymore, but we started out driving and got as far as Des Moines. We were so worried and tired that I knew I wasn't going to be able to drive all the way. So we turned around, dropped the car off at home and Traveled. I figured you would all be up by now. We agreed that this is a family situation that trumps any regulations imposed upon us by the Director. If I have to do some explaining later, I'll deal with it, but we needed to get here as soon as we could."

Hildie nodded thoughtfully and said, "I'm sure you did the right thing. I'm certain it won't be a problem, or at least not one we can't tidy up." Nona's grandparents jumped into the conversation, agreeing with Hildie as they hugged Nona's parents.

Nona listened to her grandparents ask if her parents were hungry or thirsty, while her parents peppered everyone with questions about what had gone on and what Nona had been told. Aunt Hildie pointed out the time, repeatedly. Nona couldn't help but chime in and tell her parents about her experiences since leaving home. After a few minutes of this affectionate confusion, Grandpa Fred announced that it was time to get to work, and things began to settle down. The presence and concern of her elders made Nona feel both protected and guided, which were things she realized she really needed at the moment. As the din of the mini-reunion settled down, Nona's mother asked Hildie what they had planned for the day.

"I think we have to teach Nona some of the basics," Hildie said. "She can clearly Travel, but has no control over it yet and has no idea how to get around safely or get back home again. Her powers are developing a lot more quickly than any of ours did, so she's going to have to come into her own more quickly than we did. We can get her enrolled in classes once she's able to control her abilities."

Nona saw her mother grow pale and shudder slightly. She wondered what her mother had seen in her Travels. She had made a comment about a rule against Traveling. Why had she and Dad been hanging onto each other when they arrived? Nona had never seen her mother cling to her father's arm like that. Nona found herself thinking that there was a lot about her parents' past that she didn't know and couldn't even imagine. And what was this about coming into her own more quickly than they had? There was an ominous tone to Hildie's voice as she said that, Nona thought. Nona put the questions on her mental list of things to ask. She looked around the room as Hildie and her mother continued their conversation, wondering about all five adults. Her grandparents had been at Woodstock. Her father should have died at the Battle of Culloden. Her mother had visited Scotland in the 1740s. Aunt Hildie seemed to wander around history like most people wandered around a shopping mall. None of these were things she could have imagined 24 hours ago, not even in her wildest dreams.

Just thinking the word "dreams" made Nona's mind wander to her own dreams over the last few months. The dreams had begun right after the holidays and had grown more and more vivid with time, each one haunting her for days. They were filled with places she was reading about in her literature or history classes or places she had seen in films. They were so clear to her that she could hear small sounds like ticking clocks and rustling leaves and could smell things like coffee brewing in the next room, or food on the table or smoke from a fireplace. In them she could feel heat and cold, could feel pain if she stubbed her toe and could taste food.

The faces were another matter. For several months she had been seeing faint, ghostly images of faces in the corners of rooms and in shadows. She had been afraid to tell anyone about them, thinking she was going a little crazy. Knowing that this was related to Traveling made them more frightening, not less so, she realized.

Nona drifted back into the conversation going on around her, just in time to hear Hildie explaining to everyone in urgent tones that she thought it best to start right away with Glimpsing. Nona was about to interrupt and ask what that meant when her father jumped in and said he agreed.

"For her own safety, she needs to learn to Glimpse immediately," he said, walking over to rest a hand on Nona's shoulder, his accent becoming more pronounced as it always did when he was upset. "Between the dreams, the scene at the Historical Society, and yesterday's Visit, we know she'll have the ability to Glimpse. Given the pace at which she's coming into her abilities, I think we'd be wise to prepare her to move quickly and safely and to get back home. I don't want her lost in the past for who knows how long while we blunder about looking for her."

To Nona he said gently, "Given the dreams you were having and the way you were behaving, we pretty much knew what was happening to you. Your mum and I didn't want to go into it until we were sure and until we knew how extensive your abilities would be. We thought we would have time to explain it to you and then do the normal testing. Then you had that trouble at the Historical Society and we knew we had to move more quickly than we had planned. I'm sorry now that we waited. We could have spared you the shock of Traveling unannounced yesterday."

"Sweetie, I'm so sorry that we couldn't explain this the way we had planned," her mother stepped over to Nona and put a hand beside her husband's on their daughter's shoulder. "I think it would have been much easier on you had it gone that way. Hildie warned us that she thought you were developing abilities quickly and that you were going to be a gifted Traveler, but I don't think we were ready to admit it. Coming into your abilities is a huge step. We're very proud of you and excited for you, but we're also concerned about your safety. Traveling can be dangerous."

Nona looked up into her father's face, and realized that she had never noticed the small lines etched in the fair skin beneath his deep green eyes. Nor had she ever noticed that his hair was beginning to glint with strands of gray. Her mother's face looked tired, almost severe, more so than Nona remembered it looking before. The thought of time passing had never really crossed Nona's mind before, except when she counted weeks until a holiday or summer vacation. Looking at her parents now, it felt as though she was seeing them as people, not just parents, for the first time. In the light of everything she had learned in the last day, the signs of age on their faces and the thought of them traveling through time to be together, brought a lump to her throat.

"We have a lot to talk about over the next few days," her father said, kissing the top of her head. "For now, let's just start your education."

Elaine Schmidt

CHAPTER 5

"Right, then," Nona's grandmother said, exiting the confusion and heading for the kitchen. She kept speaking, her voice growing louder the farther she got from the family.

"I've assembled a few things for us to work with. Why don't you all get settled at the dining room table." It was an order, not a question.

Nona, her grandfather, aunt and parents shuffled about the dining room for a few moments, shifting stacks of books and a jumbled assortment of Native American pots, antique hand tools and women's hats from the dining table to chairs and end tables around the dining room and living room. Each time Nona picked up something to move it, faint, floating images, smells and sounds of other times and places flitted about her. Eventually, the table reasonably cleared, her grandfather patted a newly cleared spot at the head of the table, winked at Nona and pulled the chair back so she could have a seat. Grandpa Fred always managed to create a pocket of calm in the flurry of activity Grandma Ruth created, she thought. By the time her grandmother returned, the group was just settling in at the table, with Nona seated at the head. Nona watched as her grandmother brought in the large, ornate, wooden tray that had been on the kitchen table earlier.

As her grandmother set the tray in front of her, Nona took stock of the odd assortment of what appeared to be a heap of garage sale leftovers that were piled on it. She saw a battered handbag; a dented, metal, cuff bracelet with words still faintly visible on its surface; a pearl-handled nail file; a fragile-looking teacup; a lace glove; a measuring spoon; a largish, grey and white pot shard; and a pocket watch before her grandmother sat down and nodded to Hildie to begin the proceedings.

"Nona, you must pay close attention to what we are going to teach you today," Hildie began, without so much as a glint of her usual merriment. "Travel ability is a great gift, but it's also a tremendous responsibility. You will come to realize that Travelers quite literally have the world at their fingertips in a way that most of humanity can barely dream about. But you also have the fate of the world in your hands in a way that most of humanity can't begin to fathom. There are rules – strict, unbendable rules – to which you must adhere as you visit the past. If not, you can have horrible effect on what happens from that moment on."

"You mean I can change history?" Nona asked, her eyes growing wide at the thought.

"Yes," Hildie hesitated. "You could change history, but it's not allowed. Some Travelers have tried to alter history for their own gain. They've been captured and punished for it. Others have tried to alter history for the betterment of mankind. But it never works the way they think it will. Unforeseeable, far-reaching consequences always manage to spoil what begins with the best of intentions. Those people too have been stopped and their plans undone."

"What do you mean that it never works the way they think it will?"

Hildie was silent for a moment, as though choosing her words carefully, before going on. "Think about World War II. You would think that preventing the war and all the suffering and dying and persecution would be a great thing, wouldn't you?"

"Of course."

"Well," she paused again, looking sadder than Nona had ever seen her look. She looked at Nona's parents for a moment and waited for their nods before she continued. "Great good and great evil appear in his world on a pretty regular basis and they largely balance one another out. When that balance is upset, the conflict and unrest it causes can be enough to send the entire civilized world into turmoil – and sometimes the natural world too. We had a well-meaning Traveler a few years ago who tried to prevent World War II – with the best of intentions, of course. I can't stress that enough. She believed that the war, with its horror, persecution, suffering and death was in fact the civilized world being torn apart. She attempted to stop it all from happening by keeping Hitler from rising to power in the first place.

"What she learned, what we all learned, was that without that horror, the world didn't learn the lessons of tolerance and forgiveness that followed. An evil personality still rose to prominence, although a bit later, and the world still erupted into a horrible war. But that war was longer and more devastating than the one we know as World War II. It's safe to say that not a single life was saved. In fact, more were lost."

"How do you know what happened?" Nona was both frightened and fascinated. "I mean, it didn't happen – it couldn't have."

"Ladies!" Grandpa Fred said, in a gently stern voice. He shushed Hildie with a glance before giving Nona a tender look. "You have more information to take in over the next few weeks than you can imagine at the moment. There are rules of Travel, the Society of Travelers and all of its politics to deal with, and you are going to have to get serious about learning your history and languages. We can't have you careening off into times and places that are complete mysteries to you." He paused for a moment, watching Nona's expression closely, as though he might be able to see if his words were taking root.

"But we aren't going to address everything at once, so you're going to have to trust us and be a little patient," he went on. "Everything you learn will eventually fit into the bigger picture, but if we stop to answer your every question, we'll never get anywhere, and you won't learn to enjoy what is, above all else, a very special ability. So, for the moment, let's do a little Glimpsing." He held up a hand to silence Nona as she inhaled to ask what Glimpsing meant and nodded at Hildie, as though turning over the meeting to her.

"Right. Glimpsing." Hildie said, rubbing her hands together in obvious eagerness to begin. "You've heard the expression, 'look before you leap,'" she said, not waiting for Nona's answer before continuing. "Well, when you Travel, looking before you leap into a time and place is absolutely essential. As you might imagine, you can't just go plopping into rooms full of people – not in this time and certainly not in any other time. So always, always, always, look before you leap." Hildie paused, giving a Nona a stern look, before continuing.

"Glimpsing is the simplest form of Time Travel and for some people, the only kind of Travel their abilities allow," she explained. "It's the Travel equivalent of peering in through a window instead of walking through the door. Some people Glimpse in their sleep or in their daydreams for most of their lives and never realize that they are actually experiencing a simple form of Time Travel. Other people, especially artists and writers, Glimpse on a daily basis but think of it as creativity or inspiration. They write stories that they think are their own invention, never realizing that they're writing about their Glimpsings." Hildie paused, looking at Nona with her eyebrows raised as though checking to see if Nona was following her. In that second of silence, Nona's parents and grandmother all started talking at once, offering what sounded like examples of what Hildie had just explained.

"Hey!" Hildie silenced the group and said to Nona, "Since you can obviously hone in on a time and place through an object, we are going to have you handle a few objects and learn to Glimpse their past. It will take a little practice, but once you master Glimpsing, you won't be in danger of getting sucked into the past every time you touch something old, and you'll be able to take controlled looks at the past before you decide to Travel."

Nona nodded, thinking that this sounded like a pretty handy skill. She had been gingerly tiptoeing her way around the cluttered house all morning, fearful of touching anything that might send her winging off to who-knows-where-and-when. Unconsciously, she reached up and felt for the pouch her grandmother had made for her, letting out a small sigh when her fingers found it.

"As long as you're wearing the pouch, I don't think we have to worry about you doing any accidental Traveling, so let's start with something easy," Hildie said, rummaging through the items heaped on the tray until she found a small, pink stuffed animal, which she set in front of Nona. "Perfect. You just lay your hand on it, and concentrate on it. Keep an image of it in your mind and see what happens to the picture around it. If you feel as though you're slipping back, pull your hand away. But if it happens that you Travel, don't worry, I'll keep my hand on your arm, which should hold you here, or at worst, send me along with you. Ready?"

Nona was nothing like ready. Her stomach was in a knot and her hands were balled up in tight fists. But she nodded and looked at the table in front of her where Hildie had set the stuffed animal. So much of its stuffing was missing that it was tough to make out what the animal was supposed to be, but somehow Nona knew it was a kitten. She unclenched her right hand, which was shaking just slightly, and slowly brought it to rest on the animal. Her ears immediately filled with a jumble of voices and sounds and she felt the tug of Travel an instant later. She withdrew her hand with a gasp and looked up at Hildie for instructions.

"Did you remember to keep an image of it in your mind?"

"No." Nona realized that in her nervousness she had simply reached out and waited to see what happened. She shook her head, glanced at her mom and dad for reassurance, took a deep breath and looked at the kitten a moment longer before moving her hand toward it again. This time she stared at the toy and concentrated on it as hard as she could, staring at its tattered, synthetic fur and the worn seams that had given way to spill stuffing. Finally she reached for it. The jumble of sounds was softer this time, and the tug wasn't as strong. Instead of feeling herself in the swirl of passing time, she saw time swirl around the stuffed animal in front of her. It made her a bit dizzy, but as she continued to concentrate on the toy, she began to make sense of the images before her.

Nona remained aware of the dining room, although it began to look more like an unlit backdrop for a play than like the room she was actually sitting in. In front of the backdrop was a hazy, slightly out-of-focus image of a child's bedroom. Curled up in a crib was a sleeping child. The child, who Nona assumed was a girl, given the pink pajamas she was wearing, was clutching a new version of the little stuffed kitten as she slept. Nona took a moment to look around the room and found that it was a familiar place. The windows and door and the shelves above the bed all looked like her own bedroom. Through the window she could see her own backyard, with the elaborate swing set her father had built for her when she was born. She looked at the little girl again and realized she was looking at herself in the middle of a peaceful afternoon nap. She enjoyed the happy scene a moment before slowly pulling her hand back.

"This was my toy," she said as the room returned to normal. "I saw myself sleeping in my own bedroom. I must have been about two."

"Exactly," Hildie nearly shouted as the others nodded excitedly. "I gave it to you for your second birthday. You carried it everywhere you went for almost three years, until it began to fall apart and your parents replaced it and packed it away. They brought it with them. Tell us what you saw."

"I saw myself as a little girl, sleeping in my bed," Nona said. She paused a moment before adding, "It was daytime. The sun was coming in through the window, so I guess I was taking a nap. The house was really quiet."

Hildie's eyes were shining with excitement. "Did you try to turn around and look behind you or peer out into the hallway?"

"No, it felt as though I was looking in through a window, like you said. I didn't know I could turn around."

"Let's have her try again," Grandma Ruth said. Hildie and Grandpa Fred agreed. Nona's parents suggested a break, but Nona said she felt just fine and wanted to try again. They all went silent, watching intently as Nona reached out for the stuffed kitten.

Once again, Nona heard the jumble of sounds and a slight tug on her hand as she touched the kitten. There was no fear this time, just a combination of excitement and fascination as time appeared to swirl around the toy. She stared at the kitten, concentrating hard, until she could once again see the girl, herself, sleeping with the stuffed animal. Struggling to focus on the slightly hazy image, Nona turned to look over her shoulder. She could see into the hallway outside the bedroom and could hear the muffled sound of the mantel clock chiming twice in her parents' living room. Craning her neck just a little allowed her to see into her parent's bedroom, where her mother was stretched out on the bed, clearly taking a nap herself. As she watched, her mother's eyes opened. She stared at Nona, with a startled look that slowly changed to a mix of warmth and pride. She smiled, closed her eyes again and lay very still. Nona began to pull her hand away from the stuffed animal and felt the years rush past her as she returned to the present.

"Well that was weird," Nona said breathlessly when the room and her family were back in complete focus. "Mom, I was looking at you – you were taking a nap in your room – when you opened your eyes and looked right at me. You looked like you knew it was me."

Nona's mother nodded, her eyes filling with tears. "I did see you that day," she said with a catch in her voice. "I can't as a rule see Glimpsers. But that day I felt as though someone was watching me, so I looked around and there was a dim image of a face. It startled me at first but I looked the person in the eyes and she looked back. I realized she looked a lot like Hildie when she was young, but still a little different. As I looked, I realized it was you Glimpsing me from some time in the future."

She explained that it was the moment at which she had known that Nona would be a Traveler. As Nona grew and began to look more and more like the girl her mother had seen that afternoon 11 years earlier, she knew her daughter was about to start Traveling. She had been watching for the signs for some time.

"So Glimpsers can be seen when they look in on a place and time?" Nona asked, thinking that it wasn't such a nifty ability if you scared the wits out of people every time you Glimpsed.

"Oh heavens no," her grandmother said. "Only Travelers can see Glimpsers, and not even very many Travelers have that ability. It's called Sensing. Some Clockers can Sense, but since they can't Glimpse or Travel they usually think they've seen a ghost or an alien. I often wonder how many Clockers are able to Sense but won't talk about what they've seen for fear of having people think they're a little off in the head."

"Clockers?" Nona knew her grandmother wasn't welcoming questions at the moment, but she couldn't help herself.

"Ah, yes," her grandmother said. "Technically they're called the Chrono-Bound, which refers to the fact that they're stuck in their own time and have no recourse but to follow along as time progresses. Different eras have had different slang for these people. I guess the current slang is still Clockers."

Hildie, who had just taken a swig of cold coffee and was making a face as she swallowed, nodded.

"In my day they were called The Trapped," her father said. It took Nona a moment to remember that his day was 250 years in the past.

Nona's mother explained that Nona was the only Glimpser she had ever seen, which made her wonder if the likelihood was stronger when the Glimpser was someone you loved. The family began talking amongst themselves, recalling Glimpses in which someone had Sensed them and Nona wandered off into her own thoughts. She was trying to process everything she had seen and heard over the past couple of days, but so much of what she was being told seemed awfully vague.

"Excuse me," she said finally, unsure of any other way to bring the adults back to the matter at hand. "There seem to be a lot of things you're all not sure about. Why is that?"

It was Grandpa Fred who took the helm this time. He sighed, cleared his throat and rubbed his hand across his face before saying, "Nona, the world of Travelers is complicated. No two people have the same abilities and no one person's abilities stay the same throughout their lives. Some people's abilities increase as they get older, some reach a certain point and begin to diminish. Some people develop only one or two abilities and other people develop dozens. There's no way to predict how a person will develop nor is there a way to train people to develop abilities. We can train people to control their abilities, but that's about it.

"Tomorrow we'll take you to a place that will become an important part of your Traveling life and let you see what it has to offer to people like us in the way of support and training," he continued. "Hildie," he said, turning to his daughter with an urgent look on his face. "Perhaps you should make a stop there today and make sure that tomorrow's a good day for us to go?"

"That's a good idea," she said, pushing her chair away from the table and smacking into a long, wooden sign advertising Tootsie Rolls propped against the wall. It teetered for a moment, but Grandpa Fred reached out and steadied it, propping it back up against the wall and holding it there as Hildie got up and reached for her carpetbag. "I'll be back shortly," she said. She got a blank look on her face for a moment, which Nona assumed meant she was Glimpsing, before disappearing with her trademark flash of blue light and loud bang.

"Now," her father said, as though calling the meeting back to order, "where were we?"

"Wait," Nona interjected before anyone else could get them moving in another direction. "So how did that work? I could see what was going on in other rooms just by moving my head a little. I didn't really go into Mom's bedroom, but still it's like I did."

"That's the joy of Glimpsing, dear," her grandmother said. "You're not really there, so no one, well almost no one, can see you. All you have to do is reach your mind out to the place and time you want to see and have a look and listen."

All I have to do, Nona thought. They were making it sound so simple. She looked around the room uneasily, wondering if anyone was looking at them and listening in. The couple of brief Glimpses had left her tired and hungry. But they had also left her wanting more. More than anything, she wanted to feel in control of what was happening to her. She couldn't help but think about the fact that she would never be able to tell a single one of her friends about any of this. That idea made her feel rather lonely, even in the midst of family.

"How about trying this?" her grandfather said, pulling a faded, yellowed piece of paper from the goods piled on the tray and tossing the stuffed toy back on the heap. He took a quick look at the paper before sliding it in front of his granddaughter.

Nona squared her shoulders, took a deep breath and reached out for the paper. She stopped for a moment, leaning forward to look at it first. It was a report card, with her grandfather's name on it in faded ink. She brought her hand over it and settled it in place on the age-softened paper, waiting to see where it would take her. After a few moments of swirling sounds and images, Nona found herself peering into a classroom. But it wasn't a classroom like any she knew. There were no computers to be found anywhere. A well-worn set of encyclopedias and several other books flanked one of the long windows, held upright by a battered set of metal bookends. The children all wore uniforms – the girls in shapeless plaid jumpers and white blouses and the boys in dark slacks and white shirts. A teacher dressed in a rustling, knee-length dress and clicking, high-heeled shoes, walked up and down between the rows of desks, handing out pieces of paper just like the one Nona was touching.

"Freddy," the woman said as she walked toward Nona sending a whiff of rosy perfume and stopped at a nearby desk. "Your hard work paid off. Nice job." As she walked away from the child she had called "Freddy," Nona recognized the boy from photos she had seen of him in the family albums. He was her grandfather, about 10 years old, but him nonetheless. She took a moment to look out the window and peer out into the hallway before withdrawing her hand and returning to the dining room.

"That was you!" she was staring at her smirking grandfather. "How old were you?"

"I was in the fourth grade," he said nostalgically, "and I had just gotten my first 'straight A' report card."

For the next several hours, Nona used a hatpin to Glimpse a milliner's shop full of women in fancy, floor-length dresses. A black, metal hook allowed her to see a blacksmith's shop and a heavy, white china tea cup showed her afternoon tea being served on what appeared to be an ocean liner. A yellowed baseball won her a look at a baseball game in a place called Borchardt Field, where the players wore slightly silly-looking, old-fashioned uniforms and caps. After about a dozen such Glimpses, Nona suddenly felt light-headed and leaned back in her chair. She had no idea how much time had passed.

"Lunch," her grandmother blurted, as though reading Nona's mind. She pushed her chair away from the cluttered table and patted Nona on the shoulder before racing off to the kitchen. "I'll have grilled cheese ready in a few minutes. Let's give the child a break."

CHAPTER 6

Waiting for lunch and then again during lunch, Nona's parents and grandparents told her stories of their own Glimpses and Travels, relishing the telling as though they had been waiting years for the opportunity to share their stories. *I guess they have been waiting years,* Nona thought. She wondered to whom she would tell such stories someday. Certainly none of the friends she had made so far in her life, all of whom would think she was either lying or crazy.

Interspersed with the stories were fragments of rules and odd terms that Nona had never heard before. Part of Nona wanted to interrupt the stories to ask questions, but a greater part of her was too tired. It was easier at the moment to be quiet and listen. Just as they were finishing their grilled cheese sandwiches, Nona heard the telltale hum of an incoming Traveler.

"I think Hildie's on her way," Nona said absently, eating the last crumbs of the potato chips her grandmother had served with lunch.

Her grandparents exchanged glances before her grandfather asked, "Nona, how exactly do you know that someone's coming?"

Hildie arrived with her usual bang and flash and Nona said, "The hum. You know, that low, soft hum that gets louder as she gets closer? Hildie's has a different sound than the hum that Mom and Dad made. You mean you can't hear it?"

"No, neither of us hears it," her grandfather said.

"I used to hear it, but I haven't been able to for years now," her father said as he helped clear the dishes.

"I've never heard it," her mother said, popping her head in from the kitchen.

"Me either," Hildie said. "I've only known one other Traveler that hears that."

"What does that mean?" Nona asked. The whole idea of Traveling, and the fact that she could never discuss any of it with her friends at home, was making her feel like a freak. The thought that she was odd even in this family of Travelers made her feel stranger yet.

"Sweetie, all of us have different abilities," Hildie said, grabbing a handful of potato chips from the bowl Nona's dad was carrying to the kitchen and munching them as she spoke. "Some Travelers are what's known as Apparators. They appear briefly in another time, but only partially. Imagine your mind wandering to another place and time and then realizing that, for just a brief moment or two, you're actually there. Apparators can't control their Travels – it's almost like a sudden sneeze. They're there for a moment, and they can be seen, although they're sort of foggy and translucent to the Clockers. Most Clockers see for just a second or two and then they're gone again. If you read up on ghost stories, you'll realize pretty quickly that most ghost sightings are really just Apparators letting their minds wander or Glimpsers taking a peek and scaring the bejeebers out of some poor Clockers in the process."

"They could be Hostages getting dragged to and fro," her grandmother added, shaking her head with a pained look on her face.

"That's true," Hildie said in an oddly muffled shout. She had polished off the handful of potato chips and was now digging in the fridge for something to eat. Grandma Ruth shooed her out of the kitchen and began to make another grilled cheese sandwich. As she waited, Hildie explained that some Travelers had no control over their abilities at all. Known as Hostages, these people popped in and out of times and places with no way to stop or get back home.

"Sometimes we can rescue them and sometimes they're simply lost in time," Hildie said. "They end up living like homeless people, trying to stay out of sight, stealing what they need to survive and therefore staying out of trouble."

"We? What do you mean?" Nona had a mental image of a posse of Travelers, all of them a lot like Aunt Hildie, just waiting to rush off and save some poor, lost soul from a lifetime of hopping through history.

"Let's just show her," Nona's grandmother suggested, reaching across the table to give a few gentle pats to Nona's arm. "She seems to have mastered Glimpsing. I don't think we need to devote the afternoon to more of the same. She needs to see what she's a part of in order to appreciate what we're teaching her, don't you think?"

Looking at each other and nodding in agreement, Nona's parents and grandparents turned to Hildie with questioning looks on their faces.

"Today's as good as tomorrow," Hildie said, with a quick why-not shrug.

"You're about to have an adventure," her grandfather announced to Nona, nodding and smiling enthusiastically. "We're going to take you to a place that will be part of your life as long as you Travel. It's called the Sanctuary Out Of Time, or SOOT for short. This is the headquarters of the Society of Time Travelers." He had pronounced SOOT like the word boot. Clearly excited about the adventure himself, he began organizing the expedition.

"Hildie, lock the front door, would you?" he asked.

"I'll check the back door," Nona's grandmother called from the far end of the kitchen. She had already closed the window over the sink and was already on her way to the door. "Nona," she called, her voice rising as she moved through the house, "SOOT is sort of home base for Travelers. You can never discuss what you see and hear as a Traveler with any of your Clocker friends. None of those friends can help you if you run into trouble. Because of this, Traveling can leave you feeling quite alone. SOOT is the place where you can turn for help, companionship, research and support. And the restaurant serves some of the best lingonberry pie you'll ever taste."

Nona smiled when she heard the term "Clockers" again. Although it had sounded terribly strange to her just a bit earlier, it made perfect sense to her now. These were people who couldn't Travel and were therefore bound to live their lives in chronological order, by the clock. But lingonberry? She had no idea.

Nona watched as her parents and grandparents bustled around the house getting ready to go to SOOT. Her dad unplugged the coffee maker, Hildie and her grandmother closed windows, her mother, done with the dishes, turned out lights, while her grandfather had put down fresh water for Baxter and put the telephone handset back on the charger. How funny, she thought, it's the sort of stuff you do before you go out for a picnic or a trip to the mall. But we're going to someplace that … she realized she had no idea exactly where they were going. She was about to ask when her grandfather announced that they were ready to go.

"You don't need to be nervous," Hildie said, digging in her over-sized carpetbag like someone checking for a set of keys. "This is going to be a lot like the trip you made to the Museum of Science and Industry in Chicago last year with your class. There are going to be lots of things you won't really understand and probably a lot of things you'll forget. But you're going to get a look at something that the vast majority of people in the world don't even know exists, even though it's essential to keeping their lives flowing on through time."

Nona was no less nervous after Hildie's reassurance, just more curious. She smiled and nodded at her aunt, hoping she looked more confident than she felt.

"Nona, you let that pouch your grandmother made for you rest on the outside of your shirt and take my hand. You can ride with me," her father said, holding out his hand and moving to stand beside her. "Don't you worry, even in the years since we stopped Traveling, your mum and I have remained active at SOOT and have been there often. I know the way and I'm proud to give my daughter her first look at the place."

Grandpa Fred looked at Hildie and Grandma Ruth, then at Nona's mother and father and finally at Nona herself, as though taking one last check of his team before sending them into a game. Standing as straight as Nona had ever seen him stand, he said, "What a proud day this is."

No one actually moved. What happened next was more a matter of the room moving around them. Nona watched, holding her breath, as the room shimmered and began to rush away from her, as though a bubble had formed around her and was pushing everything outward. The sensation only lasted a moment before dissolving into the same rush of sounds, smells and flashes of images that she had experienced the day before, when she was yanked into the past and then propelled back to the present. Although the whole experience was still stunning, the feel of her father's hand in hers and presence of her family made her feel much safer. She felt herself pulled forward, although much less suddenly and violently than the day before. The arrival was also smoother. Instead of plopping in a heap on the floor or smacking into a doorframe, they seemed to slow down just before they arrived. She and her father landed gently and neatly on their feet. Nona took a deep breath and realized her mother, aunt and grandmother were standing beside her, just as they had been at the house. The only thing that had changed was their surroundings – and those had changed incredibly.

Gone was the pleasant clutter of her grandparents' house. In its place was an enormous, light-filled room, topped by a great, windowed dome. The gleaming marble floors and vast space reminded Nona of one of the several state capitol buildings she had visited on family vacations. This space had the same huge-room echo as those buildings as well. All around the outside of the enormous room were tall, marble pillars positioned in pairs, situated on either side of doorways. Through each doorway Nona could see a long hallway, lined with doors. People bustled through the hallways, some carrying parcels, some carrying papers and files. In one hallway she saw women dressed in white nurse's uniforms of wildly different eras and styles, pushing wheelchairs and carrying trays of what appeared to be medications. In another hallway she saw men and women dressed in what appeared to be police or military uniforms of some sort. They hurried about in small groups, locked in intense discussions.

Nona turned to peer down some of the other hallways. In one she saw people in period costumes moving about in groups. Down another hallway were men and women in lab coats pushing carts that were loaded with an odd assortment of goods. Just in her quick glance she saw paintings, sculptures, yellowed papers, musical instruments, a fragile-looking wooden chair, a few swords, stacks of ancient-looking books and pieces of a suit of armor, all being wheeled to and fro.

Nona's father waggled his finger in the general direction of the pouch Nona was wearing. She nodded at his reminder and slipped it back inside her shirt. She was distracted instantly by the telltale hum of an incoming Traveler. As she listened, it turned to several hums and grew louder very quickly. Red lights at the top of the paired pillars began flashing in unison, which triggered a mad rush out of the center of the room. Aunt Hildie hustled Nona and her family to the shelter of the nearest pillar. Nona understood their haste a moment later, when a series of pops and flashes delivered a group of running men and women to the domed room. Stumbling and panting, dressed in what looked like 1930s clothing, they slowed to a stop, several of them losing their balance and tumbling to the floor. One of the women took a quick head count, clearly relieved at finding the number of people she expected. They collected themselves and headed down the hallway where Nona had noticed the artwork being wheeled hither and thither.

"What was that?" Nona asked, breathless with excitement. She wanted to ask about everything she had seen so far, but the dramatic arrival they had just witnessed got bumped to the top of the list.

"Those people were a team from Art and Humanities Reclamation, better known in-house as AHR or Culture Vultures," Hildie explained. "They swoop in and rescue art works, musical manuscripts, one-of-a-kind books and such in the moments before they are known to have been destroyed. SOOT has an enormous archive of some of the finest works of mankind, all of which have been saved from destruction by teams like the one you just saw."

"So there's a museum here?" Nona had always loved museums, something her family had instilled in her.

"Not so much a museum as a storehouse," Hildie said.

"So many of humanity's greatest achievements have been destroyed by wars and natural disasters," her grandmother added. "Some years back SOOT decided to make it part of their mission to save as many of these masterpieces as possible. We lose some of the past with each generation – it's inevitable. But with some of these items, we have been able to pinpoint the date on which the item was destroyed. The theory is that if it was destroyed and lost to history, then no one would notice if we grabbed it in the moments before it was destroyed and brought it back here."

"But what happens to it once it's here?" Nona understood the idea of saving precious historical artifacts, but it seemed a waste if no one ever got to see these things again.

"They're here for study and reference," her grandfather explained.

"Any Traveler who is registered with SOOT can come in and work with these items. Some of the items have been returned to the world at large, or reintegrated. I don't suppose you would remember, but a few years ago the famous Hermitage museum in St. Petersburg, Russia, announced that they had come across some paintings that had been confiscated by the Germans during the World War II era. Later they were spirited off to Russia and hidden away. When they resurfaced, the museum began the process of returning them to the families of the people who had once owned them."

"Were they saved by SOOT?" Nona felt as though a simple set of historical facts had just taken on layers of new meaning.

"They were," her grandfather said. "They had all actually been destroyed in the war, so a team from AHR saved them. Eventually, when no one from the war years who might realize something was amiss was working there anymore, the paintings were tucked into storage boxes deep inside the Hermitage. They sat there for several years before they were discovered. It was a proud day for all Travelers to see some of history's horrible wrongs set at least a little bit right."

Hildie had set off across the great room and was gesturing for the family to follow her, with a look on her face like a kid about to open a big, wrapped birthday gift. They followed her down the same hallway the Art and Humanities Reclamation team had just entered. An ornate bronze plaque on the wall bore the name of the department. Nona wanted to take a moment and walk past each hallway to see what the other plaques might say, but Hildie was clearly in no mood to tolerate dawdling, so she hurried along with her family.

Once in the long hallway, the family had a long walk past dozens of neatly labeled doors. Each one bore a word or two that made Nona want to peek inside, such as: Paintings, French; Sculptures, Greek; Literature, Middle Eastern; Jewelry, Women's; and Armaments, South American. The doors, their lettering and the incredible possibilities that lay behind them went by Nona in a blur, until they stopped at a door labeled: Folk Art, American, and stopped. Hildie, whose cheeks were flushed a bright red, either from excitement, the exertion, or the pace at which she'd led them down the hall, paused with her hand on the doorknob and said, "You are about to see one of my best finds. Mom, you especially are going to love this."

The family walked through the door to find a small, tidy counter manned by several middle-aged women all dressed in jeans and casual shirts or sweatshirts. Behind the counter was a cavernous warehouse. Rows upon rows of shelves stretched far back into darkness, each stacked with boxes and crates of every imaginable size. A woman at the counter with tousled, short, brown hair and dressed in jeans, a white blouse and an open smock, looked up and greeted the whole family with a rather cool "Mmm hmmm?" before she recognized Hildie. Her demeanor changed the moment her eyes rested on Hildie's face.

"Hildie, dear, what can we do for you?" Her face, which Nona had thought quite stern when they all entered, broke into a warm, welcoming smile as she gave the group her full attention.

"I need to see my latest acquisition," Hildie said, cryptically. "It's a bit of surprise for one of our group. Oh, I should introduce you, Meg." Hildie proceeded to introduce everyone to Meg, who very graciously shook hands and made the sort of "pleased to meet you" small talk required in such situations. She said she'd be right back, winked at Hildie and scurried off, disappearing into the rows of shelves. It was easily 15 minutes before she returned. The delay clearly didn't sit well with Hildie, who began drumming her fingers on the counter at about the four-minute mark and was pacing madly by the time 10 minutes had passed. She checked her watch repeatedly while Meg was gone and looked like she was about to burst by the time the woman returned.

Meg looked terrible when she got back. Her face had a harried, worried look. She was walking very quickly. Once at the counter, she held up a hand to silence the questions Hildie had begun to ask. She checked several log books and a card catalog and disappeared again, coming back much more quickly this time.

"It's gone," she said with an anguished tone in her voice, "It can't be gone, but it is. It can't have left this room, but it must have. Oh dear, this is the worst one yet."

Hildie's face registered both anger and concern as she asked, "How many?"

"It's the fourth missing artifact from this department that I'm aware of," Meg responded, wringing her hands and shaking her head as she spoke. "But it raises a bigger question. We found that these four items were missing because someone came in and requested them." Gesturing to the vast storage area behind her, she asked, "How many items are missing that we don't know about because no one has requested them recently? And where in time have they gone?"

Hildie reached out to pat the hands Meg was wringing frantically. "I'll look into it," she said. "For the moment, let's just keep this between us, okay?" Meg nodded, tears beginning to well up in her eyes and her lower lip quivering madly.

The family left the Folk Art, American department and stood in a huddle in the long hallway. Everyone turned to Hildie with expectant looks on their faces, but it was Nona's grandmother who spoke first.

"What's going on here, Hildie?"

"I'm not sure yet, Mom, but whatever it is, it's not good. Things have been disappearing from the various reclamations departments for weeks now. Not big things, nothing like a Monet or a Rembrandt. Just little things – like the very first *Superman* comic book that came off the presses. I asked her for the quilt that won the contest at the 1933 World's Fair."

Nona's grandmother gasped. "That's been missing for decades. You found it?"

"I did. I brought it back here and Meg catalogued it, but now it appears to be lost again."

Nona's grandmother quickly explained the significance of the quilt to the rest of the group. It was the winning entry in a contest held in conjunction with the 1933 World's Fair in Chicago. Sears sponsored the contest, inviting quilters all over the country to create an original quilt on the fair's theme, "Century of Progress." More than 25,000 entries were submitted. They were judged first on the local level, at Sears stores all over the country. Those that advanced past that level went through another, regional-level of judging. The winners at that level went on to the fair.

"But Sears hadn't banked on that many entries," Grandma Ruth explained, clearly relishing the opportunity to tell this story. "You have to remember that this was the middle of the Great Depression. All over the country families were barely getting by. Times were different than they are now. There were very few jobs open to women. If a woman wanted to work she could either be a teacher or a nurse, both of which required training, obviously. Or she could clean houses, do laundry, cook or take in ironing for a wealthy family. So women, particularly in small towns or rural areas where there weren't a lot of wealthy families to hire them, were pretty much powerless to help bring in money to keep their families afloat. They saw this as their one shot at pulling their families out of poverty."

Nona looked at her mother, grandmother and aunt and wondered what kind of people they would be if their lives were limited in the ways her grandmother was describing. In her world, women could be doctors, lawyers, astronauts and could run for president. Shaking her head at the idea of growing up in such a limiting time, she turned her attention back to her grandmother's story.

"Many of the women who entered the contest had to use scrap fabric for the quilts, because they had no money to buy anything new. Some took apart other quilts and cut up clothing to pull together the fabric they needed. Not expecting the response they got, Sears had not made the theme of the contest entirely clear to the judges. There was no national standard in the local or regional judging. Quilts were advanced in some localities that would never have been advanced in others. It came down to the personal preference of the judges in many cases and local politics in others. On the national level, the idea of a commemorative quilt about a century of progress seemed forgotten.

"Eventually, a woman named Margaret Caden won the contest. She was not one of the thousands of women who poured their hearts, souls and hopes into their quilts. She was a businesswoman, an extremely rare thing at the time, who sold, among other things, handmade quilts. It came out years after the contest that she had hired some of the women who sewed for her business to make the quilt. Those women, who could not afford to lose their sewing jobs in such tough economic times, were afraid to speak out at the time of the contest. I had heard that the winning quilt was given to the First Lady, Eleanor Roosevelt, but that no one knows where it went after that."

She was clearly excited by the idea that she had come so close to seeing the quilt. "Hildie, where did you find it? How could it have disappeared? Who would want it?"

But Hildie's attention was elsewhere. They had just reached the two pillars of the great, domed room, when Hildie stopped in her tracks and held up a hand to silence the others. All eyes were on Hildie as she scanned the great room. Her eyes came to halt and she squinted slightly as she looked down the hall containing administrative offices. Suddenly, she whirled around and ushered the family back down the hallway, urging them to hurry. The first door they came to was labeled Britain Costume, Middle Period. Hildie jerked the door open and rushed her family inside. Before Nona had a moment to take in the wonders of the large room, which was filled with tunics, dresses, armor and more ancient flotsam and jetsam than she could begin to take in, Hildie hooked a single finger on the strap around her niece's neck and yanked the pouch up and out of Nona's shirt, letting it drop on the outside of her blouse. She grabbed Nona's hand and shouted, "Home! Now!" Nona felt herself pulled into the whirlwind of Travel once again.

Elaine Schmidt

CHAPTER 7

The family members arrived at Nona's grandparents' home within seconds of each other, all of the adults talking at once again. Nona, her senses overloaded by the humming and popping of that many Travelers arriving in the house almost simultaneously and overwhelmed by the day itself, found herself tired beyond belief. The morning of Glimpsing, the Travel to SOOT and the mad dash back to her grandparents' house had taken every ounce of energy she possessed. She dropped her pouch back inside her shirt to still the sounds coming from all of the odds and ends in the house and slipped into a stuffed chair in the living room. She closed her eyes immediately.

"We have to get moving in a few minutes," Nona heard Hildie say. "I want us all to be back at our normal lives and looking completely unperturbed by all of this if anyone comes knocking."

"Comes knocking? What did you see? What sort of shenanigans are going on at SOOT these days to get you this worked up?" Nona's grandfather looked equal parts worried and angry.

"I don't know, Dad," Hildie said, pacing the floor and scratching her head. "Odd things are going on these days. You know that Don Walden was elected head of SOOT a couple of months ago. Well, he's a politician to the core. He's got a gift for schmoozing people into doing what he wants and can make them believe his promises and join in his tirades, whether or not they know what he's talking about. It's a little frightening."

"You know we've had a very hard time getting any straight answers on the disposition of a few Anasazi artifacts that were scheduled to be reintegrated in the last couple of months," Grandma Ruth said with an irritated edge in her voice. "Could that be related to what's going on?"

Hildie, who was now pacing in a tight circle, said it could. She explained that Walden had tightened security in certain areas of SOOT and was getting more involved in the day-to-day running of many of the departments than any director before him. With artifacts disappearing left and right and his unusual leadership, it was clear something was going on and it seemed as though it was either being condoned or ignored – neither one of which was appropriate.

"But it reaches further than the halls of SOOT," Hildie said. She began digging through a stack of newspapers sitting on top of the piano. "Here it is," she cried, waving a sheet of newspaper in her hand.

"I saw this the other day and didn't know what to make of it," she said. She proceeded to read a brief article about a handwritten piece of Bach's music that had surfaced a month or so earlier. "Scholars have decided that it's actually in Bach's handwriting. A man with no ties to the music world whatsoever claims to have found it in an antique shop in Germany. He sold it to a British University for $600,000. He prefers to remain anonymous. University scholars are trying to piece together the work's history, trying to determine how it landed in the German antique shop, although so far with no luck."

"That *is* odd," Grandpa Fred said, taking the newspaper from Hildie and reading the article himself, as though looking for something she might have missed.

"It certainly is," Grandma Ruth said. "These sort of discoveries are almost always made by academics, or at very least by antique dealers who are going through someone's estate and stumble upon something. I suppose it's possible, but Bach's music is so well documented and has been for so long. I don't know, it sounds odd to me."

"I don't like the fact that the person who found it is trying to remain anonymous," Nona's father added. "That's not the sort of thing you would think someone would want to hide."

"I think we all agree that something's not right at SOOT at the moment," Hildie said. She was still pacing. As the tension level in the room rose, everyone followed her movements. It occurred to Nona that the family looked as thought they were watching a tennis tournament in slow motion, turning their heads from left to right in perfect unison as she paced. But she had no time to enjoy the silly image. Hildie abruptly stopped her pacing in the middle of the room and looked around at everyone for a moment before speaking.

"We have to do something about all of this. I think I have a plan. I think Hugh and Lois should go home and go about their usual business and they should do it immediately," she said gesturing to Nona's parents. "We want things to look as normal as possible. I'm going to spend some long days at SOOT and see if I can't figure out who's involved in this. I may stake out the artifacts warehouse and see if I can't catch them in the act. Nona should probably stay here and go about spending the summer with her grandparents as planned, although being careful not to go winging off to the past accidentally. Mom, Dad, you should just enjoy the time with Nona and plan on communicating with me a few times every day. You should also work on figuring out just what Nona's abilities are and teaching her to control them. Meanwhile, Lois, you and Hugh can call here every day or two to check on Nona, which will seem perfectly normal. Does that sound good?"

"I don't know," Nona's grandfather sounded worried. "What are you going to do, all alone, if you figure out who's involved in the thefts? You don't know who you can trust."

"I was thinking that I go to the Chrono Cops and make a report on the missing quilt and maybe report a couple other artifacts Meg mentioned. I'll do it loudly in the middle of the workday, so that the whole department will hear it. They can't all be involved, now can they?" Hildie nodded to herself as she spoke, as though deciding her plan was a good one as she described it.

Nona had to ask. "What on earth are Chrono Cops?"

"Sorry honey, I keep forgetting you don't know these things yet," Hildie was trying to sound patient, but she was speaking so quickly that it was hard to catch everything she said. "Technically it's called the Department of Temporal Integrity Enforcement. Any one of the researchers or reclaimers, or basically any Traveler, who spots a temporal inconsistency reports it to them. It's the job of the Chrono Cops to track down the offending Traveler and apprehend them. Just like any society, we have rules and a system of justice to enforce them."

Nona nodded, trying to look as though this made sense. It didn't work, given that very little in her world made sense at the moment, least of all the idea of a time police force. She felt as though she was reading a long, complex novel in three- or four-page segments that were completely out of order. Someday, she thought, it might feel as though I've read the entire book and then things might make more sense.

"I'm going to gather up my things and go back to work. I have artifacts to find. I'll get messages to you as I can and will stop in from time to time to let you know what's going on. I wouldn't be completely surprised if … "

Nona had a sudden jolt of a bad feeling. She went from drowsing in the armchair to standing on her feet beside Aunt Hildie so quickly that she didn't remember what made her move so quickly at first. Then she heard it – a soft tinkling sound a little like a wind chime in a gentle breeze. A shimmer in the far corner of the living room caught her attention a moment later. Her odd behavior had stopped the conversation and had grabbed everyone's attention. Before anyone could say anything, Nona stretched her face into what she hoped was a convincing smile and waved at the image just beginning to appear in the shimmering corner.

"Hi!" she shouted at the face, plastering what she was sure was a horrible grin on her face and waving furiously. Turning back to her family she said, "Look! Someone's Glimpsing us. I think we're going to have company." As she said the last bit, she stared at Aunt Hildie who returned her stare intently. Nona hoped that her aunt understood this to be a warning. It was only a few hours ago that they had talked about Glimpsers and the fact that no one else in the family could see them. This Glimpser seemed to be lurking, as though wanting to watch and listen without being seen or heard himself. It didn't take any Travel experience at all to know that someone hiding in a corner and eavesdropping couldn't be up to anything good.

Nona looked back at the face in the corner and saw that it was a man and that his eyes had gone wide in a look of surprise or fear, or possibly a bit of both. He recovered quickly and waved back at Nona. He held up a finger, as though telling her to wait a moment. She was about to tell her family what she had seen when she heard the hum sound of an incoming Traveler. As it crescendoed she said, "He's coming." She had barely gotten the words out when the hum turned into a wet, slithering sound and ended with a soft plop and the appearance of one of the men Nona had seen walking into the great room at SOOT just before Hildie had hurried them all home.

"What luck, the Sullivans and the McDonalds all in one place," he said reaching out to shake hands with Nona's father and grandfather. He was smiling broadly, but Nona noticed that the smile didn't seem to reach all the way to his eyes, which remained guarded and serious. "Is this a family reunion? I do hope I'm not interrupting."

Hildie took a step toward him and began speaking a little too quickly and a little loudly. "No, Director Walden," she said, "you're not interrupting at all. We just got back from showing SOOT to Nona. We think she'll start coming into her abilities any day now and we want her to be as comfortable as possible with everything. We thought it would be good to show her what she's going to be a part of. Unfortunately, I think we gave her a bit much to take in. I think we've exhausted her."

Nona made a point to look tired as Hildie introduced her to the Director. Internally, Nona was kicking herself for dozing off during the adults' conversation. She couldn't remember what they had said about the Director, but she could dimly remember them mentioning him. When the introduction was over, her family members, who were normally all speaking at once, fell into total silence.

Grandpa Fred cleared his throat and asked, with overdone deference, "What can we do for you, sir?"

"Oh, yes." The Director smoothed his silk tie with a quick, nervous-looking gesture and said, "I saw you at SOOT a little while ago and wanted to say hello, but you must have left a moment later. Nothing's wrong, I trust?" He pulled his face into a credible look of concern.

"Well honestly, I was quite upset," Hildie said evenly. "I wanted to show my mother my most recent reclamation, but it's gone missing," Hildie said evenly. "I was so disappointed that I decided to head straight home."

"You reported it of course," he said, making it both a question and a statement at once.

"Actually," Hildie responded, "I wanted to make sure everyone got home first so they wouldn't have to wait around for me to finish. Hugh and Lois aren't Traveling anymore and Nona's just beginning to come into her abilities, so I thought it would be a bit much for my folks to shepherd them all back here. I was just saying that I have to get back."

Nona listened intently and realized that everything her Aunt Hildie was saying was true. She simply wasn't offering any more information than she wanted to share.

"Yes. Of course. Very thoughtful," he said. He had stopped looking at any of the family members, and had begun scanning the room and its clutter instead. His eyes lingered on several objects, longer than was polite but not long enough to give anyone else the time to turn and figure out what had caught his attention.

"Well then, I'll wish you congratulations on the potential of adding a new Traveler to the family," he said giving Nona a pointed look, "and I'll be off, as long as everything's alright."

"It is," Hildie said, to a chorus of nods across the family. "But I am irritated that I have to start searching for that quilt again."

"Oh, is that what's gone missing? A quilt?" The director sounded either unconvincing or distracted, Nona couldn't tell which.

"Not just a quilt," Grandma Ruth said, anger evident in her voice. "The 1933 Chicago Exposition grand-prize-winning quilt. It must be found."

"I'll absolutely do what I can to bring it back to SOOT," Director Walden said in an unconvincingly calm voice. "I'll keep you apprised of any developments." With that he gave a flat-handed wave to everyone and said, "I'm off," just before exiting the room with the same slithering sound that had ushered him in.

No one moved or spoke for a full minute after he left. Finally Hildie blurted, "What on earth was all of that about?"

"I don't know," Nona's mom said, staring at the space the director had just vacated. "Should we feel flattered that he came here to make sure nothing was wrong?"

"Why was he Glimpsing us? I think we should feel grateful that our Nona is a Senser," Nona's father said. "Otherwise, we would never have known he was there. Who knows what he might have heard us say?" Although his face reflected some concern, it was the incessant tapping of his left foot that offered a clue as to just how tense he was.

"Somehow I didn't want him to know that Nona has begun Traveling," Hildie said, a frown etched in her forehead. "I'm quite sure that I don't like this feeling of mistrusting the Director. Something is wrong at SOOT and I am afraid he may be a part of it."

The family began talking about the current goings-on at SOOT, but Nona was too tired to listen. The comfy chair won her over and she dozed off again. When she awoke, something had changed in the tone of the conversation.

"If we send her back, no one but us will be able to find her," she heard her father say. "She has no Signature yet, so as long as none of us Travel with or to her, or try to Glimpse her, she should be invisible to anyone at SOOT."

"I think Hugh has a good point," Nona's mom said. "I hate to think of sending her off alone through time, but maybe that's best for the moment. We can bring her home as soon as we know what's going on."

Nona was suddenly wide awake. "What did I miss?" she asked, a little fearful over the direction the conversation had taken.

Hildie cleared her throat, effectively silencing the rest of the family. She turned to Nona, pulled up a footstool and sat down to look Nona in the eyes.

"Something's not quite right at SOOT," she said, sounding as though she was weighing each word as she spoke. "This really may be nothing major. It may be dealt with quite quickly. It also may be something huge that permeates much of SOOT. In that case, I'm not sure what will happen." Hildie dropped her head and rubbed her face with the same gesture her father often used.

Grandpa Fred spoke up from across the room, where he was seated on the couch. "Nona, Travelers have tremendous freedom in their abilities to move from time to time and place to place. But Travelers are also quite vulnerable to injury and mishap as they Travel. We have to be able to trust the folks at SOOT because they're all we have to turn to if something goes wrong. It seems as though something crooked is going on there. The problem is that we don't know who's involved and who we can trust. For the sake of the entire Society of Travelers, we have to figure this out and see that it's set right."

They went on to explain that they had decided to send Nona to Winnie's time – to the house she had Visited accidentally when she had first touched the quilt. Hildie explained that while Nona was dozing, she had tidied up her costume, and Glimpsed a day in Winnie's mother's life about 12 years before Nona would arrive. She explained that she was going to go and talk to her to explain that Nona would be coming for a very short visit and then a possibly extended stay in the days after her daughter finished her first quilt. She disappeared and was back in less than a minute.

Nona's parents agreed they should go home and get back to business as usual, although Nona could see in their faces that they weren't the least bit happy about the situation. Her grandparents decided they would continue with their usual summer Anasazi excavations near their home, Traveling when they could and sniffing around discretely for information on the strange goings-on at SOOT.

Hildie would go back to her normal job, which made Nona chuckle a little since she now knew how far from normal that job was. They would use their jobs as cover while they worked on solving the problem at SOOT. They all agreed to keep in close touch with one another and try to get letters to Nona every couple of days.

"You know," Nona's mother said with a far-away sound in her voice. "I have a good friend from my Traveling days who decided to live out her life in Winnie's time, somewhere in the Philadelphia area. She set herself up in the 1870s, I believe. I'm sure we can find her. We can get messages to her and she can mail them to Nona at Winnie's."

"That's perfect," Hildie said getting a notepad and pencil out of her carpetbag and taking down the information. As she did a quick Glimpse and took off to the past to have a quick conversation with the friend in 1890s Philadelphia, Nona's parents and grandparents prepared her for life in the past. Taking turns, they gave her an enormous amount of information, most of which she knew she would never remember.

"You will want to make a homing pouch for Winnie's farm as soon as you get there," Grandma Ruth said. "You must not experiment with Travel abilities, no matter how tempting it may be. If we lose track of you from Winnie's, we may never find you again. The fact that you don't have a Signature yet will keep you safe from being found by anyone meaning to do you harm, but it will also keep you from being found by us."

"Stay in the background," her grandfather warned with a grave voice. "If you do anything that alters the Timeline in a significant way, SOOT will certainly find you."

"Be very careful not to injure yourself in Winnie's time," her mother said with a worried frown. "Medical care in rural America in those days was horrible and slow in arriving. Just be careful."

"Be careful not to talk about your time," her grandfather told her. "Many things we take for granted will sound like witchcraft to most people in the late-1800s."

"You must never let anyone see you Travel," her grandmother said. Her face became more worried with each bit of advice.

The warnings, advice and instructions went on for nearly 45 minutes, until Hildie came back from Philadelphia.

"I found her. It's all set. We did the math on dates, so that the letter we write tomorrow should be waiting for Nona when she arrives at Winnie's."

As everyone else in the room nodded and congratulated Hildie on a job well done, Nona got stuck on the details of what she had just said. "Wait a minute," she interrupted. "If I'm going to Winnie's today, how can there be a letter waiting for me that you won't write until tomorrow."

"Nona, you're thinking like a Clocker," Hildie sat on the footstool in front of Nona as she spoke. "Time is only linear for those who are forced to plod along with it. Travelers are free of the constraints of linear time, at least as far as the past is concerned."

"A practiced Traveler can place him- or herself within a few days, some within an hour or so, of any moment in history," her grandfather said, lapsing into what Nona assumed was the voice he used when lecturing his classes. "You're going to leave for Winnie's in a few minutes. Let's say it takes us three weeks to solve the situation at SOOT. When we're done we will come and get you. But time is fluid for us. We can go back to get you just a few hours after you arrived at Winnie's. It will be as easy for us to go back 122 years and three *hours* as 122 years and three *weeks*. Does that make sense?"

Nona paused before answering. "If I read it in a novel or saw it in a movie I guess it would be believable. But sitting here listening to you tell me that you're going to send me to the 1890s and that you'll come and get me in a few weeks but it will only be a few minutes – that's a pretty weird idea."

"I know it is dear, and it was a pretty weird idea for all of us once too," her grandmother gave Nona a big hug. It felt different, Nona noticed, than the one at the airport. That hug, at the airport, had been vigorous and happy. This one was serious, almost sad somehow. Nona felt sad herself at how much her world had changed in the space of just a little more than 24 hours.

"Nona, you understand that we'll try to come and get you as soon as we can. But right now we can't even Glimpse you because our Signatures might lead someone to you. We don't know that anyone is going to come looking for you. But because of your family tree, you hold the promise of developing tremendous Travel abilities very quickly. Anyone who's trying to hide his or her activities at the moment will probably see you as a threat. We just feel it's best to be cautious with you until we know what's going on."

Her grandmother warned her to keep her Glimpsing skills sharp by practicing a bit every day. Her grandfather told her to be sure and help Winnie's family, pointing out that she was about to learn how much harder people worked in past generations. Hildie warned her to keep her eyes and ears open.

"Nona, there are a few more things you need to know," Hildie said gravely. "Not all Travelers are decent, honest people. Do you remember I told you that there are people out there who try to alter the past for their own gain? Well there are two types of these criminals in the world of Travelers. There are Rogues, who steal artifacts and take them to times and places in which they can sell them and make a lot of money. They aren't interested in altering timelines; they're just in it for financial gain. These aren't the best people and they're certainly not a group of Travelers you should ever get involved with, but they're usually not dangerous. And remember, taking an artifact out of its time, unless you're salvaging it in the moments before it's destroyed, will alter any Timeline that contains that artifact in the future. Imagine if a Traveler from our time went back to steal the Mona Lisa 100 years ago. How many people have seen it in the past century? A song was written about it and people named their daughters Mona and Lisa because of it. Think how many events would be changed.

"The other group is called Opportunists," Hildie went on. "They are Travelers who try to alter the past and or the future, trying to create a situation in which they have greater power, control or money than they do in the present. The problem right now is that we don't know who or what we're up against – Rogues or Opportunists or just a bunch of wild teenagers on a lark. I don't know who can be trusted at SOOT right now and I don't know who I can tell you to trust. Just wait for one of us and avoid any other Travelers."

As Nona nodded, her aunt added, "You can hear Travelers coming, which may prove to be a valuable skill. You also seem to recognize individual Signatures, like mine. If you hear someone other than me coming, assume it's not someone you want to see and get out of sight. Just be cautious. Again, one of us will come for you in a few days. I don't know what's going on yet, but I'm sure we'll get it sorted out quickly enough. I'm sorry your Traveling life has to start out like this," Hildie kissed her forehead and gave her a big hug. "We'll all be back here in no time. I can't wait to get back to your training."

Nona nodded, feeling less sure of herself and her situation than she ever had in her life.

"Come with me, dear," her grandmother said, heading toward the back bedrooms with a purposeful stride. "We are going to get you outfitted for your trip. That t-shirt and those jeans and sneakers just won't do in Winnie's time."

As Nona stood to follow her, wondering what sort of outfitting this was going to be, she heard the sound of an incoming Traveler, coming at them fast, and gasped loudly. She was about to announce that fact when she realized she was hearing several incoming Travelers, not just one.

"People are coming," she said. The looks flashed immediately between Hildie, her parents and her grandfather terrified her. Hildie dashed to the dining room and returned in a flash with Winnie's quilt.

"Take off your homing pouch and put it in your pocket," Hildie's urgent shout frightened her into quick action. As soon as the pouch was in her pocket, Hildie threw the quilt across the living room to her and shouted, "Go!"

Nona caught the quilt and realized she had no choice but to go where it was going to send her. The sounds, smells and nauseating blur of images she experienced when she touched the quilt in the closet began again. Her family, their worried faces turning to face the incoming Travelers, disappeared as she hurtled backwards in time.

Nona landed more gently than she had the first time she arrived in Winnie's room, but not by much. Once again, the quilt from her time had not come with her, but the new version of it lay rumpled on Winnie's bed. She tried to breathe normally as she struggled to get her bearings. A cold feeling gripped her stomach as she wondered what her family was facing in the time she had just left.

Winnie wasn't in her room this time and, from the silence in the house, no one else was around either. Taking her aunt's warnings about being inconspicuous to heart, Nona decided to wait in the little bedroom for Winnie to come back. She sat down on the edge of the lumpy little bed, where it took only a few minutes for her exhaustion and the appeal of a bed and a quilt to get the best of her. Nona wrapped herself in the new quilt, pausing for a moment to ponder the fact that a few moments earlier she had touched a 125-year-old version of it, and immediately fell into a deep sleep.

***

Almost instantly, or so it felt, a high-pitched squeal pulled Nona out of a tangled web of vivid dreams. Standing beside the bed was Winnie, wearing the same astonished look as the last time Nona had seen her.

"It's you again!" Winnie's voice was shrill with excitement. "She's here!" Winnie squealed even louder, turning her head toward the door as though alerting the household. "Mother will be thrilled to meet you. But are you well?"

Nona realized that she must look a fright. She had no idea how long she'd been sleeping. Although it felt as if only seconds had passed since she laid down, at least gauging by how tired she still felt, her mouth was dry and pasty and her eyes felt scratchy each time she blinked them.

"I'm fine," she said, shaking her head to wake herself up. "I'm just really tired. It's been a long day." She had no idea what time it was or what day or date, but it was clearly sometime after her first Visit to Winnie. She remembered her grandmother saying something about Winnie wanting to use the quilt for a few days before she packed it away in her hope chest. The quilt was still on her bed so it could only be a few days at most since her last visit.

"Could I get a drink of water?" Nona asked. Instead of answering the question, Winnie stuck out her hand, not like one would if expecting to shake hands, but limply, palm down, almost as though she expected Nona to kiss it.

"My name is Winnie," she announced, with a formal tone.

Nona reached up and held Winnie's fingers for a moment, giving them a little shake for lack of really knowing what to do in response to the gesture. "I'm Nona," she said.

"Pleased to meet you, Nona," Winnie said, bending her knees and bobbing slightly. "Mother says you are a Traveler. After the last time you visited, she said you would be coming back and that I mustn't be afraid of you when you did. Today she said we had to make something called a homing pouch for you and here you are, right on schedule. So I am not the least bit afraid of you. Are you from the future or the past?" Her eyes were wide with curiosity.

"I'm from the future, although it certainly sounds odd to me to say that. Do you think I could get a glass of water?" Nona hoped the request would register this time.

"Certainly! Follow me, please." With that Winnie disappeared through the doorway. Nona followed just in time to see the girl's head disappear as she scrambled down a ladder to the first floor. Nona followed, too groggy still to take in the details of Winnie's house. Once on the ground floor, Winnie darted through the kitchen, flung open the back door and ran out into the yard. Nona stopped in the doorway, squinting hard. She stopped and looked at her surroundings for a moment, stunned to see that other than the farm buildings surrounding the little yard, there were no other buildings on the horizon. Well, she thought to herself, if Aunt Hildie wanted to hide me away, this is certainly the place for it. With no other signs of civilization in sight, Nona thought it unlikely that she would run across too terribly many people from this time. She was still taking in the scenery when Winnie ran up to her with a large ladle full of water.

"Still cool from the well – it should be quite refreshing," the girl said, passing the dripping ladle to Nona who slurped eagerly from it.

Nona sputtered after her first swallow, coughing hard for a few seconds. The water tasted like a rusty nail and was full of what felt like sand in her mouth. She sat down, hard, in the doorway and, before she could stop herself, began to sob. Everything I know is gone, she thought. Correction: nothing I know will exist for more than a century. I don't even know if my family is safe. The wave of despair that washed over her at that thought made her nauseous and dizzy. She laid her head on her lap and tried not to be sick.

"You are not well – I knew it!" Winnie went running off to one of the outbuildings, shouting for her mother. Nona was too tired, weak and heartsick to do anything but sit where she was, hugging her shins and resting her head on her knees. She wondered where her family was, correcting herself again to wonder *when* her family was. They'll come for me soon, she told herself. She found that repeating that sentence helped soothe her so she kept repeating it in her mind as Winnie and her mother bundled her back into the house and up to the loft. Mother and daughter worked side by side, cooing and clucking at Nona as they pulled off her t-shirt, jeans and sneakers and slipped a soft, cotton nightgown over her head. Nona was dimly aware of Winnie's mother placing a homing pouch around her neck and kissing the top of her head in much the same way her grandfather liked to do. Feeling cared for, if far from home, she felt herself lowered into Winnie's bed and felt gentle hands pull the quilt up to her chin. She fell into a deep sleep.

CHAPTER 8

Birds. Nona awoke to more bird sounds than she could remember hearing at any time in her life. Even camping didn't sound like this, she thought. Still, she kept her eyes closed. She knew where she was, or more to the point, where she wasn't. She wasn't at home in her own room where things made sense. She wasn't even at her grandparents' house in Durango, where things were a little odd, but still pretty much made sense. She was in Winnie's attic bedroom, which Aunt Hildie had told her was in Paola, Kansas. She was in 1898. Allowing herself to think the date made her stomach tighten into a knot of fear and tension. 1898. No one I know, not even my grandparents, will be born for 60 more years. Even if I live to be an old lady in this time, I could only get to know my grandparents as children. These were thoughts that threatened to paralyze her.

Nona sat up, quietly, and pushed back a rumpled cocoon of quilts, shivering in the chilly, damp air of the early morning. She looked around and saw a makeshift bed on the floor, feeling a wave of guilt that Winnie had been forced to sleep on the floor because of her. The makeshift bed was empty. She looked at the window, where she could see faint traces of light through the thin curtains. The sun isn't even up yet, she thought. What time do these people get up?

She stood up and stretched, wincing at the feel of the rough, cold flooring beneath her feet. She looked for her clothes and remembered Winnie and her mother getting her out of the t-shirt, jeans and sneakers she had arrived in and saying something about hiding them away so they wouldn't have to explain them to anyone. On the dresser lay a stack of unfamiliar garments with a small piece of paper that bore her name. She shrugged out of the wrinkled nightgown and stepped to the dresser.

Digging through the pile of clothes, Nona realized there was no underwear to be found. With no one at hand to ask about it, she pulled on the closest thing she could find to pants, a pair of muslin capri-length things with ruffles at the cuffs, and put them on. Realizing this was all going to take a lot of getting used to, she pulled on a white, strapped top she knew was a camisole. This *is* underwear, Nona thought, chuckling at the fact that this was already more clothing than she would wear on a normal summer day at home. She went on to figure out the rest of the items in the stack of garments.

Nona put on a long-sleeved, fitted top that was made of dark-brown fabric covered with tiny multi-colored flowers. She had a small pang of homesickness, thinking that her grandmother would call this a calico pattern. The top looked to have been hastily let out, with wide stripes of similar fabric set in at the side and back seams, as though it belonged to someone much narrower in the shoulders and waist. The sleeves, which were far too short for her arms, had tiny buttons on cuffs that Nona could see would never close while her arms were in them. Next, she stepped into a heavy, long skirt that was made of the same fabric. It too had been let out and had been lengthened, both with additions of similar fabric.

Nona tried to get into the button-up shoes sitting beside the dresser. Deciding they were impossible to button once a foot was inserted, she decided to skip shoes entirely for the moment and to find Winnie and her family. The ladder leading down to the main floor, which was steep and narrow to begin with, was almost impossible to navigate in the long skirt. Nona stepped on her skirt, lost her balance, stumbled and slid down the last couple of rungs, getting splinters on her hands and feet before landing on her behind on the floor. She had barely landed when she heard footsteps on the porch and saw the door swing open.

"Oh dear," Winnie cried, seeing her on the floor. "Have you fallen?"

Nona wondered if the term "duh" had any meaning in 1898. Of course I've fallen, she thought crossly. Why on earth why I be sprawled on the floor if I hadn't? Winnie deposited a small, wire basket full of eggs and a metal pitcher of milk on the table and began to help Nona to her feet, which proved surprisingly tricky, given the long, full skirts they were both wearing.

"Are you hurt?" Winnie's concern chased Nona's peevishness away.

"No, I'm fine. I just sort of lost it on the stairs."

"Well it can't have gone far," Winnie said, stepping over as though searching for something small. "I'm sure we'll find it in two shakes."

"Find what?" Nona asked, bending over to join in the search for whatever was missing.

"Whatever you lost, silly," Winnie said, giggling.

"I didn't lose anything." Nona checked the front of the blouse she was wearing for a missing button.

"You just said you did." She turned and faced Nona, looking worried. "Did you crack your head when you fell?"

Nona replayed the last few minutes in her head and then began to laugh.

"No, no," she said remembering the warnings about being careful what she said in this time. "'Lost it' is just an expression – a figure of speech. When I said I had lost it I meant that I had lost my balance, not that I had lost an actual thing that could be found again. You can say that if you get angry or start crying or laughing too."

"So, the 'it' refers to your temper or your composure or your balance. It's a shorter way of saying you've lost one of those things." Winnie looked pleased at having learned a new expression.

Wow, Nona thought. I've used that expression for as long as I can remember and never realized what I was actually saying. She wondered when people had adopted the expression and why. But there was no time to ponder anything right now. Winnie had already grabbed the basket of eggs and gone off to the kitchen. Nona followed, tripping as her feet got tangled in her skirts.

"You forgot your petticoats," Winnie said, seeing her trip. "She lifted her own skirt to reveal a set of slightly shorter, ruffled skirts beneath. "The petticoats will keep the skirt away from your feet. I'll show you after breakfast."

Nona thanked her, a little heavy-hearted at the prospect of putting on more clothing than she was already wearing. She felt as though she had ten pounds of fabric hanging from her body already and was dreading the heat of the day, when she was sure she was going to be miserably hot.

Winnie and Nona worked in the kitchen for about 30 minutes, Winnie explaining every step of every task patiently, with good humor. "How different is life in the future that you cannot make breakfast?" she asked at one point.

Nona explained that breakfast was the same, but the tools for making it had changed a fair amount. She looked at the enormous coffee grinder with its pretty oak casing and side-mounted, black, cast iron crank, and thought that just explaining an electric coffee grinder and a Mr. Coffee would take the better part of the morning, let alone venturing into Pop Tarts or Fruity Pebbles. It's as though I speak a foreign language, she thought, setting the table with a sense of relief that at least plates and utensils were pretty familiar in the 1890s.

"Everyone's coming," Winnie announced, pushing Nona toward the treacherous stairs. "You'd better put on some petticoats before you embarrass the men."

"How would I embarrass the men?" Nona looked down at the yards of fabric covering her legs, wondering what could possibly offend anyone's modesty.

"The skirt is clinging to your limbs," Winnie said, reddening with obvious embarrassment herself.

"Limbs?"

"There," Winnie made a vague gesture in the general direction of Nona's knees.

"My legs?"

Winnie gasped and clamped a hand over her mouth. From behind her hand she mumbled, "Oh dear, you must never use such language again. Never!"

Nona scrambled up the ladder, holding the hem of her skirt in one hand, and sat on Winnie's bed for a few minutes to take in the strange morning she had had so far. She found herself shaking her head at the fact that "leg" was apparently a bad word. She pulled on two of the three petticoats sitting on the dresser. She was ready to descend the stairs again when it occurred to her that she would probably be better off erring on the side of caution rather than running the risk of offending someone. She put on the last one and wriggled her feet into the button-up shoes, leaving them unfastened. Feeling trapped by the amount of clothing she was wearing, she inched her way down the treacherous ladder.

Breakfast was a learning experience too. A small hoard of men and boys, all wearing gritty work clothes, sat down to eat. Winnie and her mother, with some uncertain help from Nona, delivered big bowls of food to the men. It took Nona a few minutes to figure out that the group was made up of hired hands and their sons, with Winnie's father at the head of the table. The bowls the women delivered flew around the table, with each man and boy heaping scrambled eggs, sausages and fried potatoes onto their plates. Their plates loaded up, they bowed their heads in unison and muttered an unintelligible prayer that was led by Winnie's father and punctuated by a quick "Amen." On that cue, they began shoveling food into their mouths. When their eating slowed, Winnie's father gave orders for the day. The crew at the table received their instructions with nods, gulped down their coffee – even the boys, Nona noticed with wide eyes – and then pushed away from the table to get to work. Each of them said "Thank you, M'am," and nodded in the direction of Winnie's mother before stepping through the door and pulling on their sweat-stained hats. Winnie's father lingered a moment at the table, taking just a moment to give Nona a warm smile and a wink before following the men out to the farmyard.

Only after the men were gone did Winnie and her mother make any move to sit down and have their breakfast. Nona joined them and the three ate the last of the meal, which was barely lukewarm now, sitting amid the clutter of the men's breakfast. It occurred to Nona that by the time they got the breakfast dishes and pots and pans cleared away, it would be time to start cooking lunch for the men. She thought about her parents, sitting and chatting over breakfast with the morning news murmuring from the little television set on the counter and felt homesick. The thought of her grandparents, sitting at the kitchen table eating jelly toast and reading the newspaper, stopping every so often to peek over the top of the sections they were reading to share a news bit with each other, brought on another wave of homesickness. She hadn't really had time to worry about her family yet this morning. Now that she had a moment of quiet, the worry came flooding back.

"Nona, dear, what's troubling you?" Winnie's mother asked with a concerned look on her face. Nona looked around to make sure none of the hired hands might still be within earshot before she answered.

"I'm really worried about my parents and grandparents, Mrs. … ummm … ," she said, realizing with a jolt that she had no idea of the last name of the people who had taken her in.

"First of all, why don't you call me Aunt Edith from now on and call Winnie's father Uncle Ernst. I realize we are your great aunt and uncle several times over, but I should think that still counts." She patted Nona's hand with a motherly gesture that made Nona relax a bit.

"Aunt Edith," Nona said, taking care to imitate the woman's pronunciation of "aunt," rhyming it with "taunt" instead of "can't," "as I was leaving to come here, I heard the sound of an incoming Traveler, or Travelers, I'm not entirely sure which." As she spoke she reached up unconsciously to feel the Homing Pouch her grandmother had made for her 125 years in the future. The little packet, and the promise it held of getting her home, was the only things that kept her from panicking. Instead, she felt an unfamiliar pouch hanging inside her dress and remembered that Aunt Edith had given her a new pouch the night before. She patted the deep pocket in her skirt and felt the pouch she had brought from her own time, and felt the tiniest bit better.

"Your family knows that you are here and safe with us. We shall have to trust them to sort things out in their Timeline and we'll go about life here for a few days to see what happens. Remember, you don't have a Signature yet. It's going to take a little time, once things have settled down for them, for anyone to find the exact moment you arrived. If nothing happens in a few days time we shall think about taking matters into our own hands."

The wave of relief that passed over Nona was enough to make tears well up in her eyes. She thanked Aunt Edith and hiccupped a few times before she got control of her emotions. She was still worried and was more than a little fuzzy on Aunt Hildie's explanation of the passage of time for Travelers. She had thought there would be a letter waiting for her at Winnie's. She knew she was just going to be worried, at least for the time being, and would have to learn to live with that for a while. She spent the rest of the day scrambling to keep up with Winnie and Aunt Edith as they cleaned up the breakfast dishes, prepared dinner, which is what they called their noon meal, served it to the men and boys and then sat down to eat the leftovers. They cleaned up those dishes, started a big pot of soup for supper and then turned their attention to doing some laundry, which they called washing.

If I ever get home, there's a lot I'll never take for granted again, Nona thought an hour later as she was bent over a tub of hot sudsy water scraping smelly, stained work shirts against a metal washboard. She had thought doing without a dishwasher was tough that morning, although the time spent in the kitchen with Aunt Edith and Winnie turned out to be quite pleasant. But the laundry was another matter altogether. It was sweaty, backbreaking work.

First they had to haul three large, battered metal tubs off the porch and into the yard. Next they had to haul big tin buckets full of water from the pump in the yard to the kitchen stove to heat them. Once the water was nearly boiling, they toted the steaming, sloshing kettles of water from the stove to the tubs in the yard. They shaved some hard soap into the water of the first tub and stirred it up with a long plank that was worn smooth and bleached a pale gray by years of stirring laundry. They left the other two tubs soap-free, to use as rinse water. They did several batches of clothes without changing the water, starting with white things like pajamas, shirts, petticoats and camisoles. Then they progressed to dirtier clothes, the women's blouses and skirts and the men's underwear, before tackling the men's work clothes, which were the dirtiest of all. The women's clothing was hung on clotheslines they strung up in Winnie's room, which Winnie explained was "for modesty's sake." The men's and boy's clothing was hung outside to dry. Aunt Edith quizzed Winnie on German words as they worked, with Nona making wild guesses now and then, which always brought the three of them to tears with laughter.

They divided the labor, Winnie and Nona taking turns scrubbing stains and rinsing and hanging the items to dry, while Aunt Edith threw dirty clothes into the soapy water and stirred them. Working in the sun, even on a day that was relatively cool, Nona was roasting under the layers of clothing she was required to wear. She wanted nothing more than to tear off the layers of sweaty fabric. Her hair, which Aunt Edith had pinned up in a knot at the back of Nona's head that morning and called it a "bun," was wringing wet with sweat and plastered to her head.

Supper that evening was soup and bread. Once again, the men ate first, this time without Winnie's father. He did a few last chores outside and then ate his meal with Aunt Edith and the girls. By the time the family sat down to eat, Nona was so tired from her day's work that she could barely sit up straight to eat. Her hands were so sore from wringing out wet clothing that she could barely hold onto her spoon to eat the soup they had made. As she looked around the table, she could see the same weariness on the other faces as well. Winnie's father, who reiterated Aunt Edith's instruction to call him Uncle Ernst, looked as though he might fall asleep at any moment. Very few words were spoken.

The hired hands, she had learned, slept in the bunkhouse, which was apparently in one of the out buildings Nona had noticed from the back door the day before. They worked long days this time of the year, Monday through Saturday, as the crops were going in the ground. The rest of the summer they worked on their own places, coming back to help Uncle Ernst with the harvest in late summer. Most of them, Aunt Edith had explained, had small plots of land with a shanty or a tent set up to house them through the summer. As they made money, they planted crops and tried to get a year-round house put up – usually just a one-room place. When they had saved enough money, they would add on rooms, just as Winnie's father had done.

Once dinner was cleared away and the girls climbed up to the attic bedroom, Nona pulled off her layers of clothing with lightening speed and slipped gratefully into her borrowed cotton nightgown.

"All this clothing is hard to get used to," she said to Winnie, wondering the moment she said it if she had divulged too much about the future to her new friend.

"I know you cannot tell me much about the future," Winnie said, perched on the edge of her bed, looking curious enough to burst. "But I have noticed that you and Miss Hildie wear very strange garments when you come for a Visit. I hope I get to Travel one day so I can see some of the things you have seen."

"I haven't seen much," Nona confessed, grateful for the opportunity to stretch her tired back on her sleeping mat, having given the bed back to Winnie. "I didn't realize you knew Aunt Hildie. I'd only just started to Travel when everything went wrong. I don't even really know what went wrong, but nothing's like it was … when … "

The next thing Nona was aware of was Winnie nudging her awake in total darkness. Nona rubbed her eyes and squinted as Winnie lit the small lamp on the crate/table beside her bed. Some Time Travel occurs without any special abilities, she thought, like the kind that lets you drift off in mid-sentence and wake up hours later without any awareness of the time that's passed. She shrugged off Winnie's nudges and felt herself slip back into slumber. But Winnie was apparently not going to give up.

"We had better hurry," Winnie said, slipping easily into her undergarments and dress. "We have to gather eggs for breakfast."

After a quick stop at the outhouse, so far Nona's least favorite thing about 1898, the girls stumbled by lantern light into the chicken coop. Winnie showed Nona how to reach under the birds to feel for eggs, but when a chicken took a nip at Nona's wrist, she shrieked and jumped backwards, upsetting the whole coop. The two girls groped their way through the cloud of feathers and dust the birds had raised and stepped outside into the chilly, still-dark barnyard. Winnie led her to the barn, pulled the heavy door open, shutting it again behind them once they were inside.

"We'll wait in here until they calm down and forget about us. It is best to get out of their sight for a bit if you ruffle their feathers," Winnie said, carefully placing the lantern on a workbench. "Whatever you do in here, make certain not to topple the lantern. It could burn the entire barn to the ground in a great hurry."

"Gotcha."

"What?"

"Oh," Nona realized Winnie was questioning her choice of words. "I understand. I guess it can't screw up the future to tell you that we use lots of slang in my time."

Winnie asked for a few examples. Nona asked for a moment to think and began making a mental list of possible words, trying to select ones that didn't require explanations that would divulge too much about the future. She couldn't use the expression "wired," as in "I'm too wired to settle down" or "I'm wired for sound" because Winnie had no idea what wiring was nor what it might be used for. She had just settled on a few harmless expressions when she heard a sound that sent chills running down her spine. It was the unmistakable hum of a Traveler heading her way.

CHAPTER 9

"Do you hear that?" Nona grabbed Winnie by the arm and led her behind the low wall of an empty animal stall, detouring for a moment to blow out the lantern.

"Hear what?" Winnie whispered in the dark.

"A Traveler, incoming. Shhh."

The two girls huddled, trembling, in the stall. Small streaks of light around the door and at the shuttered windows of the barn told Nona that the sun was beginning to come up. She pulled Winnie closer to the floor and pressed her hand over the girl's mouth as the hum grew louder and exploded into a bright flash and a crackling pop. From Winnie's startled jump, Nona knew she would have cried out and given them away if her mouth hadn't been covered. Stunned by the bright flash in the dark barn, Nona had a hard time making out the shape of the Traveler who had just arrived. She hoped whoever it was would have the same difficulty seeing at first too. She kept her hand over Winnie's mouth, for safety's sake, and Winnie didn't resist. Listening closely for any sound that might give them a clue as to who had just arrived, both girls jumped slightly when they heard a loud sniffle and a moan.

"No, no, no," came the quivering voice of a boy. "Not again."

They listened intently as the Traveler made his way to the door, around which the streaks of light were getting a little brighter. It sounded like he was crawling, Nona thought. She pressed her face to the boards of the stall wall in order to take in as much of the barn as possible through the tiny gap in the boards. She spotted him, a boy on all fours, crawling straight for the door.

She moved her hand from Winnie's mouth and made a soft "shhh" as she strained to get a good view of the Traveler. The boy stayed on the ground and shoved the door open just a hair to peer outside. He took a quick look and scrambled back into the barn, his eyes darting from corner to corner. Nona grabbed Winnie's wrist in case they had to run to avoid being cornered in the stall by him, but he turned and scrambled in the other direction before she could get ready to move. He pressed himself between the barn wall and a wagon that was sitting on its side for repairs, and began to sob.

"Stay here," she breathed in Winnie's ear.

Nona stood, very slowly and as quietly as she could. The boy's sobs drowned out any noise she might have made. She took a deep, although shaky breath, and called out, "Hello – don't be afraid. I'm a Traveler too."

The sobbing stopped with a wet gasp. Nona realized that she was holding her breath. From the silence coming from Winnie's direction and from behind the wagon, she thought Winnie and the Traveler must have been doing the same thing.

"I'm not going to hurt you. I'm a Traveler too. My name is Nona. What's yours?" Nona's heart was pounding in her ears. She hoped she had not just done something stupid.

"Henry Sanchez." The boy's voice sounded terrified. After a great, sniffling intake of air he asked, "Where and when am I?"

Nona had never heard that particular question before, "when am I," but she knew the jolt of being plopped into a foreign time and knew the fear he was feeling.

"You're in Kansas in 1898, but this isn't my time. I came here from Colorado in 2011." Nona listened, first to silence, then to the sound of the boy crawling. In the growing light she could see his head appear at the side of the wagon.

"Really?" He peered out timidly.

"Yes. I don't belong here either. Where and when are you from?"

"I should be in Santa Fe in 1976," Henry's voice quivered, as though thinking of home was more than he could bear.

"Are your parents Travelers?" Nona thought perhaps a little conversation would help calm him down.

Henry hesitated before replying. "We took a couple of vacations, to Rocky Mountain National Park and to Mount Rushmore, so I guess we're travelers in the summertime."

Nona had a bad feeling about Henry's situation. "Do you know how you came to be in this barn with me?" She knew what he was going to say.

"No." The sobbing started in earnest again. "I was in the library at school, doing homework. I was looking at pictures of London during the Blitz in a book and all of a sudden it was like someone jerked me out of my chair and threw me into the picture. The next thing I knew I was sitting in the gutter in the street in the rain and I didn't know what to do. So I hid in an alley and pretty soon it happened again. I don't think I'll ever get home again and my parents will think I ran away." The last sentence had turned into a wail. Nona ran across the barn and knelt down beside Henry to shush him as much as to make him feel better.

"You're a Traveler, Henry, and so am I. We'll find a way to get you home," she said, hoping she wasn't giving him false hope.

"Really?"

"I promise."

At that, Henry curled up and fell fast asleep.

"Winnie," Nona called urgently across the barn. Winnie popped up in the stall, both hands clamped over her mouth. The barn had gotten light enough that Nona could see the shocked expression on Winnie's face. "Please get your mom or dad to come out here and don't let any of the hired hands in. We can't let the men see Henry yet."

Winnie, clearly stunned by everything she had seen and heard, dropped her hands and shook her head vigorously. "We can't let anybody see him. He's an Indian!" She glanced nervously at the door.

"What?" Nona stared at Winnie and realized she was perfectly serious. "What difference does that make?" She looked at the sleeping boy and wondered if he really was Native American or if he was perhaps Latino.

"Papa won't have an Indian on the farm – I know it. He'll just have to go," she said nervously, making shooing motions with her hands.

Nona was dumbfounded. Henry had no idea how to control his Travels and might never develop that ability. For the moment at least, he was what Aunt Hildie had referred to as a Hostage. Nona knew he wasn't going to develop any abilities lurching headlong through time and hiding from anyone he might come across. She also knew that even though her own training had just begun and had been hasty at that, she could at least teach him what she knew. First, she had to get Winnie into her camp.

"Winnie, I know I'm not in my own time and I know I shouldn't attempt to change things in this time, but I just have to help Henry and you're going to have to help me." Winnie opened her mouth for what Nona was certain was going to be a protest, so she held up a hand to silence her new friend. "In my time it's just plain wrong to treat someone differently because of their race. I don't care if he's Native American, Mexican or Martian, he's in trouble and we're going to help him."

Nona sat on her haunches and thought for a moment about the racism still alive in her own time. She wondered how many years into the future she would have to Travel to find a world without it.

Turning her thoughts to Henry, she decided the most important thing for him was to be able to stay put for a while. She knew that if he went winging off through time again she would never see him again and he would probably never get back home.

"Winnie," Nona said gravely, "we have to make an homing pouch like mine for Henry and we have to do it right now before he slips away. We are going to need some fabric, a strip of leather or a shoelace or some string, some sewing supplies and some flowers that are just opening this morning.

Can you get those things for me? Quickly?"

A very pale Winnie nodded and slipped out the door, drawing it shut carefully behind her. Nona settled in beside Henry and held on to one of his arms. She didn't know if it would work, but it was all she could think to do to hold him in this time until the pouch was ready. She stroked his hair with her other hand, muttering, "Poor guy," and imagining what it would have been like if she had not been able to get back to her grandparents' house after her first trip to Winnie's room – and worse, what it would be like to be jerked, helpless, into a new place and time every few days or hours. She was beginning to understand why Aunt Hildie, her parents and her grandparents had kept talking about how serious Traveling was.

A few minutes later, the door opened a crack and Winnie backed into the barn, her hands and apron pockets full of the odds and ends Nona had requested. "I told the truth," the breathless girl said with flushed cheeks. "I explained that we ruffled the chickens so we decided to make me a homing pouch just like yours for me while we wait for them to settle down. Just so it's not an untruth, we had better make me one."

Nona agreed, thinking that having a homing pouch for Winnie wasn't the worst idea. Nona quickly cut and stitched the two pouches and straps, filling them with a couple of little pieces of barn wood and the flower petals she had collected. She hoped with all her might that she was doing this all the right way, or Henry would almost certainly disappear. She had no idea how she would ever be able to help him if he Traveled again. She made an identical one for Winnie.

She woke Henry again, handing him the pouch and saying, "You must always wear this inside your shirt, touching your skin – always!" The echo of her grandmother's words brought hot tears to her eyes. "Keep it against your skin and it should keep you from Traveling. If you pop off to another time, open it and stick your finger in it to touch the contents. Concentrate hard on this place and it should bring you back here. It may not bring you back to this moment, but it can't bring you back any earlier because the flower petals didn't exist before today."

She turned to Winnie and handed one of the pouches to her saying, "We can't be too careful. You must always wear this inside your dress or blouse." As Winnie gravely donned the roughly made necklace and tucked it into her dress, Nona reached for her own two, taking comfort in the soft, small packets under her dress. She wasn't clear on whether it was okay to wear two, but if something pulled her to another time she wouldn't have Winnie's quilt to use to get back here and wasn't sure she could go to her own time without the pouch her grandmother had made for her. Nona asked Winnie if there was someplace Henry could hide for the time being – someplace no one would be likely go for a few days.

"The hay loft." Winnie said after a momentary frown. "We have used up the hay from last summer and the cattle are eating fresh greens now. No one will clean it out until late in the summer, when we get close to the harvest. I sneak to the loft to read sometimes in the summer. No one will find him there." She looked both proud of her idea and nervous. From her frequent glances over her shoulder toward the door, Nona guessed Winnie was uncomfortable about deceiving her parents.

"The hay loft it is!" Nona said with more cheer than she felt. "Are you hungry or thirsty?" Henry shook his head and explained that he had just eaten half a pie before his last travel. Nona remembered how exhausted she had been when she arrived and saw dark circles under Henry's eyes. She wondered how long it had been since he had felt safe and had had a good sleep. She spotted some burlap sacks in a corner of the barn and pulled out a few for Henry to sleep on and under. She fluffed up the remainder so no one would notice any missing and handed them to Henry.

"We'll bring you some food as soon as we can," she promised, not at all certain how that was going to work. "Just stay up on the loft until we come for you." Henry nodded and thanked her before he disappeared up the ladder. The girls could hear him working his way deep into the loft and making a little nest out of the remaining hay and the burlap sacks. As she and Winnie left the barn to make a second try for the eggs, Nona realized that feeling sorry for Henry had made her feel a little less sorry for herself.

***

"So, I hear you met the chickens," Uncle Ernst said to Nona in the kitchen an hour later. Aunt Edith and the girls were just finishing breakfast when he came in to chat with them privately. With all of the workers sharing the table at mealtime, personal conversations were few and far between during planting time and, Nona guessed, during harvest time too. She had thought him terribly stern at first, almost grim. But in the few moments of private conversation the day allowed, she began to see a charming, gentle man who enjoyed a good laugh and was clearly very fond of his wife and daughter. His face, tanned a leathery brown, was almost a shock in contrast to his bright blue eyes and the stick straight blond hair that was kept under a hat when he was out in the sun. "Did they draw any blood?"

Nervous about the secret she and Winnie were keeping from him, Nona shook her head and told him that they had scared her, but not injured her. He cautioned her to be very careful about cuts and scrapes. "I do not know much about the time in which you live, but here a cut can kill you as sure as a bullet." He nodded for emphasis and returned to the table with the workmen. Nona could hear him giving orders for the day. She remembered her grandmother talking about infections being deadly in the days before antibiotics and nervously inspected her hands for any broken skin. Finding no damage, she eavesdropped on the men's conversation, relieved when there was no mention of cleaning out the hayloft.

In addition to the daily task of meal preparation, it seemed that the previous day's washing was to be the current day's ironing. Aunt Edith set up an ironing board on the back porch and showed Nona how to keep one of the cast iron bases for the iron heating on the top of the stove, while using the other one to iron the clothes. Nona smiled, realizing that she had never given a single thought to the word "ironing" for pressing wrinkles out of clothing. She was instructed to sprinkle a little water on the clothing and press the fabric smooth until the cast iron base grew cool. Then she was to go to the stove and swap the bases, using the release lever on the wooden handle section to accomplish this without burning her fingers. By the time that base grew cool, the one on the stove would be hot. She thought about her own time with yet another pang of homesickness, remembering that she had only seen her mother iron clothing once or twice.

Although Nona wasn't thrilled about the heat of the iron and the heat of the stove, in which she was assigned to keep a good fire going, she was grateful to be positioned on the back porch, where she could keep a watchful eye on the barn. Her heart raced every time one of the workers or Uncle Ernst went in to get something, but they never seemed to be aware that there was someone sleeping up in the back corner of the hayloft. As she ironed, Nona pondered Winnie's reaction to Henry. He had dark hair and dark, brown eyes and his skin looked deeply tanned. She couldn't imagine that Nona's parents would shun the boy because of his hair, eyes and skin. But the only people she had met so far in this time appeared, judging by looks and accents, to be of Norwegian or German descent. Contemplating the situation and what to do about Henry made her realize again how very different this time was from her own and brought another powerful wave of homesickness.

Nona and Winnie managed to get some food scraps out to Henry over the course of the day. He seemed to need sleep more desperately than anyone Nona had ever encountered. Both times they brought him food, he woke up long enough to eat and then fell back to sleep immediately. Nona was a little worried that he was sleeping too much, but she had no way to do anything about it at the moment. She knew she had to get through the day's work and the evening with the family before she would be able to take a few minutes to talk to Henry when she went out to use the outhouse before going to bed. After the supper cleanup was done, she talked to Aunt Edith about trying to Glimpse her grandparents' home.

"I'm really starting to worry," Nona said. "We're coming up on day three and I haven't heard a thing from home. They were pretty sure it would only take a day or two to sort things out. I think I would feel better if I could just see that things were fine at their house, or at my parents' house. I just wanted you to know what I'm planning in case something goes wrong."

The adults agreed that Glimpsing her grandparents' and possibly her parents' homes was prudent. Aunt Edith spoke about her own Travels for the first time, explaining that both she and Uncle Ernst had Traveled as young adults, but had lost that ability after they married and had Winnie. She said her mother had had the same experience and had always assumed that one passed the ability to one's child and then could no longer Travel one's self. Nona wished her own Travel training had gone beyond bare basics and made herself a promise to pay close attention to every speck of information she was offered when things returned to normal. The thought of "normal" brought a lump to her throat. Who knew what "normal" would be after all of this?

As Nona pulled herself together so that she could concentrate on the Glimpse, Uncle Ernst drew the shutters and locked the doors, muttering that they didn't need the workmen seeing something they shouldn't. With that done, Winnie and her parents sat down around the table.

Nona explained that her ability seemed to be centered on touch, but that she had to try and concentrate and see if she could at least Glimpse without an object to touch. She closed her eyes, imagined the dining room as she had left it. She tried not to focus on her grandparents or Aunt Hildie, who she assumed would not be there. She concentrated on the room, on the mountain sun streaming in the windows and the pleasant clutter that was always a part of her grandparents' home. As she thought about it, she felt the room begin to spin around her and felt the gentle tug she knew meant it was working.

Nona opened her eyes, expecting the homey clutter and confusion of her grandparents' dining room. What she saw instead made her gasp loudly, which jolted her back to the farmhouse table and the alarmed faces of Aunt Edith, Uncle Ernst and Winnie.

Elaine Schmidt

CHAPTER 10

"What on earth is wrong?" Aunt Edith reached out and took her hand protectively. "What did you see?"

"It's trashed. It looks like it was ransacked. I need to look again." Nona knew she was speaking quickly and loudly, but she was panicked. What if someone was there, hurt? She had to take a good look. She closed her eyes and tried once again to Glimpse the dining room. Winnie and her family fell silent and watched her intently. Their faces were pale and their eyes were wide.

Her second look at the house was only slightly less shocking than the first. Nona struggled to maintain her concentration, as she took in the mess. Several dining room chairs lay on their sides, the stacks of papers Grandpa Fred had so carefully shuffled around a few days earlier were strewn all over the room. Turning her head, Nona could see that the kitchen and hallway were equally disordered. She knew her grandparents would be just sick about the mess. They could live with clutter, they even thrived on it, it seemed. But this kind of mess and the violence that created it were another matter entirely. Nona knew that the fact that nothing looked as though anyone had made the slightest effort to tidy up meant that her family had either not seen the mess yet or had fled while it was happening and had not been able to come back.

Looking around as much as she could, Nona noticed that the doors and windows were still closed and appeared untouched. She also noticed that the television and stereo and the computer were still there and the wooden box that contained her grandmother's good silver was also where it belonged, on the sideboard in the dining room. She felt slightly sick, knowing the mess had not been caused by someone breaking in to steal something. The mess had something to do with her grandparents and Aunt Hildie.

Nona shook her head and let the image of her grandparents' house fade away. The expectant faces of Winnie and her family came back into focus in front of her. Still a little dizzy, she tried to explain what she saw to Winnie and her family. "The house is a complete mess, but nothing is stolen, at least not that I can see. The TV, VCR, DVD and CD players are all there and so is their PC. But I can't see into the bedrooms, for some reason, and there is so much stuff strewn around that someone could be sprawled on the floor and I might not know it unless I was walking through the room. I have to go take a look. Someone could be hurt."

Winnie and her parents all began talking at once, alternately discouraging her from Traveling and quizzing her about all of the initials she had just used. Nona's thoughts, still a jumble from Glimpsing and the shocking scene she had tried to take in, turned to the fact that she had just divulged an awful lot about future technology, or at least about the names of future technology. No, she thought, just the initials – I guess we use an awful lot of initials for things. She had used initials like DVD so often that the syllables felt like a word on her mouth, not like separate letters. As her head cleared, Nona knew she had to go back, no matter how worried Winnie and her family might be. Her family might be in trouble. Before she tried to go back home, she had one item of great concern to deal with in Winnie's time.

"Uncle Ernst," Nona took a deep breath before continuing, "There's a boy hiding in your barn." Winnie's face contorted into a look of absolute horror, which Nona tried to ignore. "He's a Traveler, a Hostage actually, and he's at least part Native American or maybe Latino. He arrived this morning and we bedded him down and gave him some food. I either have to leave him with you or try to take him with me, but either way, you need to know that he's here." Winnie looked as though her eyes were about to pop out of her head. But, much to Nona's surprise, Aunt Edith and Uncle Ernst looked only mildly surprised by the revelation.

"Why didn't you tell us immediately?" Uncle Ernst said, sounding a little peevish and a little hurt.

"He's Indian!" Winnie blurted loudly. "You would have made him leave."

Uncle Ernst shook his head and smiled at his daughter. "No, little one, I would have done the same as you. I would have hidden him from the workmen and fed him a meal. Travelers learn early on that there are no real differences between people of different races and different times. We all want and need the same things in life and we all have a duty to help one another. Unfortunately, one can't really explain that to Plodders."

"Plodders?" Winnie and Nona said the word in perfect unison.

"Yes, those who cannot Travel and are forced to plod through time, hour by hour and day by day. Do you call them something else in your time?" he asked Nona.

"We call them the Chrono-Bound, or Clockers, but I think I like Plodders better." Unburdening herself of the Henry secret and finally talking to Uncle Ernst and Aunt Edith about Travel made Nona feel as though at least one of the huge weights she had been carrying around had been lifted from her shoulders.

"I'm sure the workmen are sleeping by now, and even if one of them is awake, none of their windows face the yard. Let's bring your new friend into the house and give him a good hot meal," Uncle Ernst said, pushing his chair back from the table. Then we will work on getting you back to your grandparents' house for a quick visit."

Nona was so relieved she could barely speak. She and Winnie tiptoed through the still night to the barn, trying not to make any sounds that might wake the workmen. She checked that the outhouse was empty before entering the barn, and watched Winnie place the lantern safely on a bench before calling, "Henry," in a whisper. "It's me, Nona. Henry, are you awake?"

A soft rustle of hay from the loft above let her know Henry was there before he called back in a timid whisper, "Yes."

"Come on down, everything's fine. Winnie's parents know about you and are going to help you." No more sound came from above. Nona tried to imagine how frightened Henry must be. "Henry, you have to trust me. These are good people. They've been helping me and they will help you too. Please come down." After a moment of silence, the rustling began again and Henry's head appeared at the edge of the loft.

When Nona got Henry into the house, she could see that he had been awake and had been crying. His eyes were puffy and red and tear tracks ran down his dirty cheeks. Nona noticed for the first time that Henry smelled as though he hadn't had a bath in a very long time, which made Nona wonder just how long he had been careening helplessly through time.

Uncle Ernst immediately set everyone in motion. He announced that the boy would need a bath and a meal – in that order. He also told his wife that Henry would sleep on the floor of their bedroom for the time being and would need some clothing in the morning. He left the room, saying he would find a nightshirt for the boy to wear after his bath. Aunt Edith, Winnie and Nona hauled the copper bathtub into the kitchen and began heating buckets full of water. With that underway, Aunt Edith ran to the root cellar under the back porch to find a jar of canned vegetables to create a quick meal for Henry.

Henry, who was more awake than Nona had seen him all day, took in the bustle with fascination. He still seemed stunned by his surroundings, which made Nona remember that no one had ever explained anything about Travelers to him. Wide-eyed, he silently took in the house and its inhabitants, fixing his gaze on detail after detail, turning to take in the entire scene the way one would take in a museum exhibit.

After his bath, which he wouldn't take until he was promised that Aunt Edith and the girls wouldn't be popping in to offer help, Henry downed several slices of bread, a large helping of soup and a small mountain of canned plums. Nona and the adults peppered him with questions as he ate, asking how long he had been Traveling, how many places he had been, how long he seemed to stay in each place and so on. Winnie listened, taking it all in with a combination of wonder and enlightenment on her face.

Henry explained his sudden departure from the school library, adding that his subsequent Travels seemed to happen when he looked at old photos or imagined a place or time. It had happened once while he was sleeping, which made him wonder if a dream had sent him on his way. He had very little idea when or where he had been, other than that he had turned up in factory of some sort, an alley, the baggage car of a train and so on. He began to talk about his family and the fact that they didn't know what had happened to him and would think he had run away or been kidnapped. This brought on a wave of shuddering sobs that sent Uncle Ernst on a sudden trip to the porch, wiping his eyes with the back of his hand as he left. Aunt Edith, who had been sitting beside Henry at the table, pulled him into a motherly hug and cooed, "There, there," for several minutes.

With Henry's wails calmed to intermittent sniffles, Aunt Edith turned to Nona and said, "Winnie's father and I have both Traveled. We had marvelous times Traveling when we were younger, before we lost the ability," she said wistfully. "It's funny, but my grandmother said the same thing to me when I began Traveling and I remember her sounding as though she envied what I was going to experience. I didn't understand it then, but I do now."

Nona took this in, filing it away as she had with much of the information Aunt Hildie and her parents had given her. More than anything, she wanted to go home and sip a cup of hot chocolate with her own parents and talk to them about their Traveling days and her Travel abilities. The more she thought about it, she just wanted to go home, to sleep in her own bed and to have a normal summer with her friends. Instead, she was sitting in a kitchen with her own ancestors, more than a century from where she should be. It was time to go home.

Winnie, her parents and Henry sat around the table with Nona as she pulled her homing pouches out of her bodice and let them dangle like pendants against the fabric. She took a quick Glimpse, following Aunt Hildie's advice to always look before she leapt. As Winnie and her family faded into the background and her grandparents' house appeared before her eyes, Nona found the same shocking disorder she had Glimpsed a little earlier. Instead of pulling back from the Glimpse and returning to Winnie's house, she concentrated with all her might and reached a hand forward toward the dining room table. She reached out to the tray of odds and ends her grandmother had prepared for her to use in first Glimpses. The tray was upside down now, the items scattered around the table and on the floor. As Nona reached out she heard and saw the now-familiar rush of years passing by. Knowing she was careening toward her grandparents' table, she forced herself to lean back, slowing her passage. Much to her amazement, her passage through time slowed, making the blurred images and sounds almost distinct. She had no time to try and slow her passage any further before she landed suddenly, on her feet this time, in her grandparents' dining room. Calling for her grandparents and Aunt Hildie, Nona quickly picked her way through the mess littering the front rooms of the house and down the hall toward the bedrooms.

Her grandparents' room looked as though a tornado had torn through it. The mattress and box spring were flung off the bed at odd angles to each other. Dresser drawers were either hanging open with contents tousled or strewn on the floor, their contents part of the general rubble in the room. Nona dropped to her knees to look under the bed and oddly angled mattress and box spring, but no one was there. She made her way through the office and the sewing room/spare bedroom she had been occupying, but there was no sign of anyone in the house. Her fears of finding someone injured in the mess were replaced with fears that her family had been taken away by whomever ransacked the house. The nagging feeling that something was very wrong, which she had hoped would disappear if she found no one in the house, grew stronger rather than weaker. It took a moment to realize that the feeling wasn't what was growing stronger – it was the hum of incoming Travelers that was growing.

Nona didn't hesitate. She sprinted back to the dining room, nearly falling on a small pile of Tootsie Rolls that had clearly scattered when the candy dish that had held them had hit the floor and shattered. Tripping and trying to right herself, she made it to Winnie's quilt laying crumpled on the floor and reached out for it. Desperate to get out of there as quickly as she could, she leaned into the confusion of Travel and braced herself for what she knew would be a bumpy ride and landing. She felt, rather than saw, the table in Winnie's house, smacking her hip into the side of the table as she appeared. She reached out for a chair, but only succeeded in toppling it and its neighbor as she fell herself.

"Nona," she heard Winnie cry out. Winnie and Henry rushed to her side, tugging her arms in opposite directions as they clumsily tried to get her to her feet.

"Nona has returned," Winnie called toward the back of the house, where Nona remembered that Aunt Edith and Uncle Ernst would probably be making up a sleeping mat for Henry. Nona shushed her friend in horror, listening to the same sound of incoming Travelers she had heard a few moments earlier in her grandparents' house.

Her thoughts racing, Nona tried to make sense of what was happening. Her family wouldn't chase her through time. They would arrive gracefully and quietly in the barn or some other secluded spot and then knock on the door. A group of Travelers that seemed to be chasing her was wrong. She recalled her Aunt Hildie telling her she should always trust her instincts. Now nearly frantic with the knowledge that she had only seconds, Nona looked around the room for an escape but found nothing. She began groping in her mind for something, anything that might provide a destination, but all she could come up with was the Tootsie Rolls she had stumbled over a few minutes earlier. With nothing else popping to mind, she closed her eyes and imagined the Tootsie Rolls with all her might. As the slightly dizzying feeling of Glimpsing washed over her, Nona found herself peering into a tiny, old-fashioned candy shop in rather dim light. Seeing no other choice, she opened her eyes and pushed Henry and Winnie away from her.

"I have to go," she said. She checked frantically for the pouches and found them dangling outside her clothing where she had left them. She closed her eyes to concentrate on the store she had just seen and let herself Travel. Nona felt herself begin to move through time again, but slower this time as though something was slowing her progress. It took a moment to understand that Winnie and Henry were clinging to her arms, passing through time and space with her. Their trip was short, barely a few seconds, and their landing was rough. They arrived in the tiny, dark shop in a rolling tangle of arms and legs, each bumping their elbows and knees on the rough wooden planks of the floor several times and emitting a brief chorus of "oofs" and "ows" in the process.

"What have you done?" Nona cried as they skidded to a halt.

CHAPTER 11

Nona squinted into the dim light, looking around the small room and trying to make out some sort of details. The air was thick with aromas: the heavy scent of maple syrup, the sharp tang of dark chocolate and the vague mingled scents of taffy and burnt sugar. She knew she was in the candy store she had Glimpsed a few minutes earlier. What she didn't know was when they were, or where the store was located. As her eyes adjusted to the dim light filtering in through the words painted on the shop's broad front window, she could see that there didn't seem to be any electric fixtures in the place. The air was chilly and, under the sweet smells, she could detect the gentle odor of wood smoke that she had grown accustomed to at Winnie's house. A squat, broad figure beside the front window made her jump and gasp slightly when she first spotted it. Staring at it for a moment, she quickly determined that it was a pot-bellied stove.

"Where are we?" Henry's voice was shaking.

"We're in a candy shop, although I don't know where it is. More important than that, I don't know when we are," Nona said crossly. She was about to let them know how foolish they had been to grab hold of her as she Traveled when Winnie surprised her into silence.

"We're in 1897 and we're in New York City," Winnie's voice was high and chirpy with excitement. "This store belongs to Mr. Hirschfield. He has a funny accent and he is selling something he calls the Tootsie Roll and it's really popular here in New York."

"How on earth do you know that?" Nona was as surprised by Winnie's announcement as by anything that had happened to her over the past few days.

"I dreamed about this place," Winnie said. "I've been dreaming about a lot places for about the past year. The dreams are so real that I can smell and taste things. When it's cold in the place I'm dreaming about I wake up shivering. When it's hot in my dreams I wake up all dewy, even if my room is cold. I fell down in my dream a few weeks ago and woke up with a bad bruise. Mama says it's my Travel ability developing."

"Dewy?" Henry was distracted from his worries for a moment.

"Sweaty," Nona said, watching Henry nod his head in understanding and Winnie wrinkle up her nose and frown at the word.

"In my dream I could see the latest fashions and I knew from the calendar what the year was," she continued.

Nona looked at her companions, noticing that their faces looked almost ghostly in the dim light. This is great, she thought. I'm sitting in 1897 with someone who dreams the past and someone who can't keep himself from getting yanked off to strange corners of the past. I'm the only one who can remotely control my ability to Travel and I've had no real training.

The three Travelers sat in silence for a moment, Henry and Nona staring at Winnie and Winnie looking from one to the other, her eyes wide.

"We're a fine team," Nona finally said, thinking to herself that they would be lucky to survive the day, let alone stay ahead of Travelers who were looking for them. Thinking about whoever seemed to be looking for them gave Nona a queasy feeling. Who were they and how did they know where she had gone? Why hadn't anyone from her time been in touch with her? Now that she had left Winnie's house and time, her family wouldn't know where and when she had gone. That thought made her feel even worse. She had to figure out what to do next, but she needed time to really think things through. Doing chores at Winnie's house had left her too exhausted to give anything very much thought. Sitting in a candy store, it didn't seem like today was going to provide any time to ponder the situation either. As she mentally chewed on these problems, Nona noticed that it was getting easier to see her companions. The sun was coming up.

"We have to get out of here," Nona whispered to Winnie and Henry. "It's going to be light soon and surely someone will come along to open the shop." They both nodded. Winnie looked excited, which made Nona wonder if she had ever been off the farm for any length of time. Henry had a determined look on his face, which made Nona feel a little better. He seemed as though he was starting to get a grip on what was happening to him rather than just cowering from it. Maybe it was just having companions that made the difference, she thought, knowing that it would be much more frightening to be going through all of this alone.

The three Travelers crept to the window, staying on all fours to avoid being seen by anyone who might be passing by. Outside, just a few people could be seen on the street, none of them very well dressed and all of them walking with the weary, purposeful strides of people going off to do a long day of work. Nona ducked away from the window and whispered, "Let's see if there's a back door," which set the trio crawling toward the back of the shop.

There was a back door, but they didn't get to it. As they were crawling into the back of the shop, squinting because the already dim light was even dimmer the farther they got from the front window, they heard the horrifying sound of a key in a lock. Nona jerked her head from side to side and spotted a small, crowded storeroom ahead and to her right. Leaping to her feet and stumbling over skirts and petticoats, she pointed to the room and hissed, "Hurry up." Her companions followed in a flurry of banged knees and elbows.

The little storeroom was full of wooden, freestanding shelf units that were stacked with tins, jars, various paper-wrapped parcels and large cloth sacks stuffed to bursting that were marked "sugar" and "flour." Several crates and barrels were positioned near the door. Nona assumed the room was full of candy-making supplies, but had no time to investigate. She was about to warn her new friends to hide when she caught sight of Winnie wedging herself between a stack of crates and the wall. Henry had darted deeper into the room, tucking himself in on a bottom shelf of one of the shelf units. Nona, the tallest of the lot, squirmed into a gap between some other stacked crates and the wall. As they each did a quick glance to locate their companions, they heard the front door open. No one needed to remind anyone else to be quiet. They all hunkered down to take up as little space as possible and listened closely.

The front door of the shop creaked as it swung open. They could hear someone stomp his or her feet and then wipe them carefully, as if trying to remove all traces of the street from their shoes before walking into the shop. It was Mr. Hirschfield, Nona guessed, as he began singing with a strong German accent.

"After ze ball vass oh-fer," he sang softly, to himself. Every now and then he would insert a line of lyrics in German. The three Travelers could hear his every movement in the quiet shop, as he walked to the front, opened the raspy door on the potbellied stove and made his way back through the shop to collect some firewood from a small stack Nona had seen near the door to the storeroom. Nona listened carefully as he moved about, tense as a cat ready to spring and trying to piece together some sort of story to explain their presence.

Still humming the same tune, the man walked back to the front of the shop and began working on lighting a fire in the little stove. Nona motioned to her companions, cautioning them to wait and to be silent with a finger to her lips. She forced herself to leave her hiding place and, pale with fright, tiptoed to the door of the storeroom. Nona took a deep breath, summoning what courage she could muster, and peered cautiously around the doorframe. In the front of the shop she could see a slight-built man, still wearing his coat and hat, working on lighting the fire. He was bending at the waist, tearing bark from the wood pieces and stuffing them into the stove. He was facing away from the storeroom and the dark recesses of the shop, with his face to the front window. Noticing how bright the light coming through the window had gotten, Nona decided this might be their only chance to get out of the shop unnoticed. She looked back at Winnie and Henry, pointed toward the back door and motioned for them to follow her.

Henry and Winnie were right behind her in a flash. They were so close to her, that when she stopped to slip the back door open as quietly as possible, they bumped into her and pushed her against the door, making a fairly loud thud. They all froze, no one daring to turn and look back into the shop. But the humming and fire-building sounds seemed undisturbed. He hadn't noticed, Nona thought. There was no time to waste. She turned the doorknob and pulled slowly to open the door as quietly as possible. Cold, somewhat foul-smelling air greeted her. Pulling the door open a little more, just enough to slip through sideways, she darted out of the shop and held the door still as Henry and Winnie followed. Nona gestured for them to keep moving away from the door once they were outside, pulling gently to shut the door before taking several quick steps away from it. She moved to what felt like a safe distance from the door before taking a good look at her surroundings. The three Travelers were in a deeply shadowed, narrow alleyway that stank horribly of rotting garbage, animal life and things that Nona didn't want to think about. The relief she felt at being out of the shop made her knees wobble for a moment as the foul smells made her stomach churn. She sat down on an upended crate to steady herself and get her bearings.

Nona had barely settled herself on the wobbly crate when a fat rat darted out from the crate, bumping into the side of her left foot and running over her toes as he escaped. Nona screamed, joined by Winnie, who spotted the rat just as he ran out from under Nona's skirt. Henry let out a staccato shout and jumped back as he spotted the rat running off. Within seconds the door to the candy shop flew open and the man who had been building the fire in the stove came charging out with the stove's ash shovel raised high as a weapon.

"Vat iss goink on here?" he barked in a thick German accent. He took the Travelers in with a glance and then squinted as he looked up and down the narrow alleyway, as though expecting to find someone lurking in the shadows.

"We saw a rat," Henry blurted, pointing in the direction the rodent had run. "A big one."

"Ja," the man said, lowering his shovel, "und you vill see vorse den dat if you play in this place." He squinted at them now, frowning at the pale, shivering trio. "Haf you been here all ze night?" he asked gesturing to the alley with his ash-covered shovel.

"Most of the night," Nona said, coming as close to the truth as she could.

"Come, Kinder, I vill give you somesing varm to eat and you vill sveep my shop, ja?" The Travelers looked at each and then at him, nodding in unison. Without a word, they each knew that they had no better plan for the moment. As they followed him back into the shop, they got their first good look at it in daylight. Even lost, scared and worried as they were, the sight of the shop made them all grin.

To Nona, the shop looked like the perfect museum rendition of a turn-of-the-century candy shop. Big glass jars lined every shelf and counter. Each jar was filled with hard candies, gumdrops or chocolates, with flavors or descriptive names written on paper labels that were glued to the outside of the glass. Hungry now, Nona's mouth watered as she read words like peppermint, sassafras, cinnamon and root beer. She turned, reading label after label, stopping when she noticed a handmade placard sitting beside the cash register at the center of the counter.

"Tootsie Rolls!" she said, startled to find one of her own favorites so far in the past.

"Ja, you know from Tootsie Roll already?" the man asked, looking rather proud. "I invent Tootsie Roll last year. Make me very famous." Introducing himself as Herr Hirschfield, he told them they could have Tootsie Rolls for dessert after they ate breakfast. He pulled four wooden chairs from a back room that appeared to hold the business workings of the shop and cozied them up to the little stove. After settling the Travelers on the chairs, he produced a loaf of bread from under the store's main counter, along with a sausage and a hard block of cheese. He told the trio to warm themselves at the little stove as he made up three large sandwiches for them. As they ate, thanking him with their mouths full, he made a pot of coffee on the stove.

The Tootsie Rolls he offered them for dessert were the best Nona had ever tasted. They were softer, less glossy and more fudge-flavored than the ones she knew in her time. Warm, fed and chewing on a Tootsie Roll, Nona was enjoying listening to Herr Hirschfield humming and clattering around the shop, getting ready to make a batch of something that apparently required a great deal of dark chocolate. When a loud pounding sounded at the back door, she jumped to her feet in fear, choking momentarily on the Tootsie Roll she was eating. Winnie and Henry were on their feet a moment later. All three Travelers began to move toward the front door.

"Do not vorry," Herr Hirschfield said, gesturing for them to sit back down. He gave them a concerned look over the top of his glasses, patted his head to smooth out the slightly-graying, dark hair that still looked as though he had just taken off his hat and tugged his vest down over a slightly protruding belly. "Milch und eggs have arrived," he called out as he walked to the back door. While he signed for the milk and eggs, and apparently butter and cream as well, another deliveryman appeared behind the first one. This man asked Herr Hirschfield a couple of quick questions that the Travelers couldn't quite hear before returning with two big, perfectly square blocks of ice. He had one block dangling from each arm, gripping them with what looked like giant, metal pincers. As Herr Hirschfield dealt with his deliveries, the Travelers huddled near the stove whispering a plan for what to do next.

"We have to find a place where we can talk," Nona murmured to her companions. "We can't just hang out in a candy store eating Tootsie Rolls forever, although it is tempting."

"We should thank him then and be on our way," Winnie said properly, before popping another Tootsie Roll into her mouth and adding a mumbled, "It does seem a pity to leave, though."

"I think we have to make a plan," Henry interjected, his own mouth stuffed with Tootsie Rolls and a film of brown fudge staining his lips. "I want to go home and so do you two," he looked at Nona. "We have to figure out what's going on and get to someone who can help us deal with it."

"I have a bad feeling that we're the only ones we are going to be able to trust," Nona looked up to see Herr Hirschfield returning from the back of the shop. "Let's get going."

The Travelers swept the floor, as promised, and then explained that they had to be going, which brought another raised eyebrow from Herr Hirschfield.

"Ver you stay?" he asked, looking from one to another as he waited for an answer. When no one spoke up, he said gently, "You remember ver I verk." He packed them a bag of bread and sausage, throwing in a handful of Tootsie rolls and gave it to them saying, "I hate to sink of my Tootsie in a cold alley. You come back to me if you need help. I am here every day."

"Tootsie?" Nona asked.

"Ja, my little daughter. I name my candy for her. Make her famous too." Herr Hirschfield patted them each on the head as they left the shop and watched from the doorway as they made their way down the street. They turned and waved once, before turning the corner to walk down the cross street.

"Wow, we really are in New York City," Henry said, pointing at a boy selling copies of the *New York Herald* on the street corner. He walked close to the boy and took a quick look at the stack of papers at his feet. As they walked on, he told his companions that the date was March 18, 1897. "You were right, Winnie," he said with awe in his voice.

As Winnie blushed in answer to Henry's comment, Nona realized that getting away from Herr Hirschfield's shop hadn't provided the relief she had hoped for. Sitting beside his stove, she had thought she would feel better, freer somehow, when they were on their own, but now that it was a reality, she was more than a little worried. Three kids who had never really been on their own in their own times were wandering a time and place they knew very little about. As she began to take in her surroundings, amazement chased her worries away.

People were walking every-which-way through the streets, stepping aside as horse-drawn vehicles of every imaginable size and shape rumbled by. Cars, or at least what Nona knew to be predecessors of cars, careened through the people, animals and horse-drawns, honking what sounded like old-fashioned bicycle horns to clear a path. The cars, which Winnie was thrilled to point out as "horseless carriages," were flimsy, rattling contraptions that were open to the air like a buggy, leaving drivers free to shout at pedestrians to get out of the way. Several pedestrians shouted "Get a horse!" back at the drivers.

Nona glanced at her companions and saw Henry gaping at the various moving vehicles, while Winnie was fixating on all the shops and windows. For her own part, Nona could hardly take her eyes off of the people. She was amazed by their clothing – by its complexity, its variety, the vivid colors of some of it and the way everyone's clothing screamed out the wearer's social status. Some people wore their wealth and power with as much confidence as they wore their perfectly fitted, richly-textured clothing. They strode down the sidewalks and crossed the streets without looking to the right or left, clearly expecting others to make way for them. The people who were dressed in clean, tidy clothing of simple cloth, moved deferentially out of the way of the well-dressed, and darted across the streets tentatively, keeping their eyes on oncoming vehicles. The people who slouched and shambled along in torn, dirty clothing moved as though they were invisible, which was just how they appeared to be treated. They made her think of the homeless people she had seen more than 110 years in the future.

Thinking of the future distracted Nona from the jumble of people, languages, smells and sounds that made up New York City in 1897 and made her realize how little she really understood about history. She glanced at Henry and Winnie, making sure they hadn't gotten separated, and it occurred to her that she didn't really know either of her companions very well either. She was just beginning to give in to growing feelings of uncertainty and dread, when Henry spotted the river and called out, "Let's head for the water. We'll find a quiet place and figure things out."

When they arrived on the banks of the Hudson, Nona was appalled by what they found. There were no paths or benches, as she would have expected in her own time. Instead, the riverbank was strewn with trash and the water itself thick with pollution, oils, sewage and floating, swollen animal carcasses. She looked at her companions to gauge their reactions and found Winnie looking up and down the river's edge, frowning and wrinkling her nose in a classic look of disgust. Henry seemed less fazed by the mess, although completely fascinated by everything around him. She thought about his world and recalled an earth science class about the pollution of the 1960s and 1970s. She wasn't sure of the date, but it seemed to her that it would have been during Henry's time that the Cuyahoga River in Ohio got so polluted that it actually caught fire.

Henry scouted out a spot for the trio to sit and talk. He chose a small, flat area on a rise above the riverbank. A bank of shrubs provided a screen between them and the bustle of the city, while the height of the rise put some much-appreciated distance between them and the stench of the river. Even so, when he held up the bag Herr Hirschfield had given them and asked if anyone was still hungry, they all agreed that the smelly riverbank was no place to think about food. Once everyone was settled in, Nona sat, head down, looking at her hands, wondering just what they were supposed to do. When she looked up, she found Winnie and Henry facing her with expectant looks on their faces, as though she had just called a meeting to order.

"I feel responsible for you two being here and I feel responsible for helping my family and now yours too, Winnie," Nona said. Gulping to keep from crying, she continued. "I want to get you both home to your parents before I try to figure out what's going on with my family. Winnie, we know that you can dream and ride along when someone else Travels. We don't know if you can Travel on your own. If I Glimpse your house to make sure no one else is around, I should be able to take you back there with no problem. Henry, it'll be a little harder with you, because I don't actually know anything about where you come from. I was thinking that if you describe it really well to me, maybe I can Glimpse until I find it and then take you back too."

No one spoke for a moment, as the three companions contemplated this idea. It was Henry who spoke up first.

"If you can take me back home today, then you should be able to do it tomorrow or the next day or even next week, right?"

"I guess," Nona wasn't altogether sure that she would be able to find Henry's home or the right time to take him back, but it was certainly not going to be any easier or harder in a day or a week than it would be right now.

"Ooooh, me too," Winnie said, grinning at Henry. "You can take me home in a few days just as easily as right now, yes?" Nona nodded in agreement.

"And since we're talking about Traveling through time," Henry said, leaning forward with a hopeful look on his face, "you could take me back a few minutes after I left and no one would ever miss me and worry, right?"

"It makes sense," Nona said, letting her voice trail off as she thought about it. "I don't know that I could manage it, but I'm pretty certain my Aunt Hildie or my grandparents could do it."

Henry nodded solemnly, saying, "Alright then, we have the beginning of a plan. We'll stay with you and help you figure out what's going on and what to do about it. You've got to be safer with us here than you would be if you were alone. When we're done you'll take us home." He and Winnie shared a glance and gave a purposeful nod in perfect unison.

"First things first," he continued. "If we were doing survival training, we would start by figuring out what we have as assets and what we need to survive. So let's figure out our assets."

"We have a bag of food," Winnie said pointing at the sack on the ground between them.

"We have someone who has offered to help us too," Nona said, thinking of Herr Hirschfield's kindness.

"We have our little pouches," Winnie added. The reminder of the pouches made Nona's heart beat a little faster.

"We need to make pouches for this place and time right away," Nona said, suddenly feeling frantic to get it done. Not knowing what any of their abilities were, or worse, what they might become, it occurred to her that any one of them could easily pop off in time without intending to and have no reliable way to get back here.

Nona used her teeth to tear strips off of her petticoat, which she knew would have inspired a stern reprimand and a lecture on tooth care from her grandmother. As it was, she was getting horrified looks from a blushing Winnie. Nona worked quickly, creating three rough, knotted versions of the homing pouch she had first seen her grandmother make just a few days earlier. She filled them with dandelion petals and scraps of paper from the sack Herr Hirshfield had given them. She reached in the sack and pulled out a Tootsie Roll, tore its waxed-paper wrapper into three pieces and placed one piece in each sack, before tying them shut and handing one to Winnie and one to Henry.

"Here," she said urgently, "put these on, wear them under your clothing and don't take them off for anything. If something happens to separate us, grabbing one of these and concentrating on this time and the candy shop should get us back to Herr Hirschfield's." They all slipped the ragged homing pouches over their heads and tucked them inside their clothing. Following Nona's lead, Henry and Winnie took the other pouches, which they were all still wearing outside their clothing, and slipped them into a pocket.

"We have Nona's Travel abilities," Henry said, returning to the task of listing assets and pointing at Nona. She frowned in response.

"I'm not sure that's much of an asset," she said hesitantly. "I've only been at this a few days and don't really know what I can do. I've only been to SOOT once and the visit ended with us fleeing, which began all the rest of this."

"What's suit?" Henry asked. "Maybe it would help us if you could explain what you know."

"There are all sorts of rules about what you can and can't say to people in the times you Visit, but I don't even know what those rules are. I'm not sure what I can and can't tell you."

Henry looked out over the dirty river, with a deep-in-thought look on his face. He scratched his head vigorously, making a patch of his glossy, straight, black hair stand up. A smile appeared on his face and he turned back to the girls.

"We are both Travelers," he said gesturing between himself and Winnie. "I hop from time to time whether I want to or not and Winnie has been having the sort of Travel dreams that apparently turn into actual Travel eventually. Since we are both Travelers, it seems to me that you should be able to confide in us without breaking any rules. You think?"

Nona thought about this logic for a moment before agreeing that it made perfect sense. She took a deep breath and told them what had happened to her, beginning with the dreams she was having a few months ago in Milwaukee and ending with the quick exodus from SOOT and then again from her grandparents' house. Tears ran down her cheeks as she talked about her parents and their Travel history, and again as she talked about the last time she saw Aunt Hildie and her grandparents. When she finished, she felt an almost physical sense of relief, as though she had been struggling to carry a heavy load and had just been allowed to set it down for the first time in a long while. Her companions were silent for several minutes, both frowning as they concentrated on making sense of the story.

Henry spoke first, turning to Nona. "Okay, now tell us what you know about Travel – the rules and how it works."

This story was easier for Nona to tell, since it didn't involve delving into her fears for her family. Nona explained the rules as she knew them and talked about the things that didn't make sense to her as well.

"One of the things I really wanted to ask about is this idea of not being able to Travel to the future," she said, her tears dry now. "Apparently, none of us can Travel to the future. Yet my mom was able to bring my dad into the future and he has been here … uh, there … ever since. I don't understand how that works. Does that mean that I can take you two to the future with me? Does it mean that you'd be stuck there?"

The group fell silent once again as each of them contemplated the complexities of what Nona had said. They were each so intent on their own thoughts that none of them heard the footfalls in the brush coming toward them on the riverbank below. The sudden appearance of a grimy, sneering face that appeared between Winnie and Henry shattered their individual thoughts with no warning. The little group froze. The face was mostly covered in dirty, matted hair, some from a long dark beard and some just plain hair that was hanging across his forehead and along the sides of his scowling face. He was dressed in ill-fitting layers of what appeared to be cast-offs. From the three hats layered on his head to the various, mismatched, torn gloves layered on his hands, and the tattered, untied boots on his feet, he was covered in a grimy patchwork of mud, grease, moldering food, and general filth.

"I'll take yer food or I'll take this little dolly," he snarled, grabbing one of Winnie's shoulders with a claw-like hand.

Elaine Schmidt

CHAPTER 12

Henry moved first. He rolled onto his back, his knees pulled close to chest. He paused for barely a second, as if taking aim, before straightening his legs and landing his feet in the center of the stranger's chest. Taken by surprise, the filthy stranger grunted as Henry's feet forced air from his lungs and sent him tumbling backwards down the riverbank, landing with a heavy, wet, slapping sound in the river mud below. Curses drifted up to the friends as Nona scrambled to her feet, grabbed a terrified Winnie by the arm and yanked her up off the ground. Henry rolled to his knees, grabbed the sack of food he had pretty well squashed flat when he rolled over and yelled, "Run!" He waited, watching the riverbank, while the girls gathered up their skirts and began to run back to the streets they had explored earlier. Henry followed, glancing over his shoulder several times as he ran.

Once they were back into the teeming streets, the shaken Travelers slowed to a walk, panting and checking over their shoulders. Nona spotted a shop with a bench in front of its window and pointed it out to her friends. The bench was empty and could be seen by anyone on the street, which made it feel like a safe haven to her. The three sat down heavily on the bench and watched the street for any sign of their attacker.

"How did you learn to do that?" Nona asked Henry, when her heart had stopped its wild pounding.

"Karate lessons," he said with obvious pride. "My mom wouldn't let me play football but my dad thought I needed a sport, so he signed me up for Karate."

"Karate? Sometimes you two talk about things that make me feel like you're speaking a foreign language," Winnie said, her frustration evident in her voice. "It makes me wonder what on earth your time must be like to be filled with so many strange things."

"Your time is pretty weird to us too, you know," Henry said. "It's like we're living on the set of a television show." Nona shook her head in a vigorous warning to Henry, but he didn't seem to catch on.

"See? There you go again," Winnie, still shaken, was nearly pouting.

"Winnie, you're right," Henry said in a calm, serious voice. "Karate is a foreign language word. It's Japanese. In my time it's a martial art that's popular for physical fitness training and self defense."

"Or for defense of your friends," Winnie said, with quick glance back toward the river.

"We've got to find someplace safe and figure out what to do next," Nona said, cutting off the conversation before Henry began describing too much of his time to Winnie. The appearance of the stranger on the riverbank had made her realize just how vulnerable they were in this time and place. "Let's go back to Herr Hirschfield's alley. It's horrible, but at least he's there if we have trouble." As they stood to walk back to the alley, she realized her legs were still shaking with fear. We've got to get out of here, she thought, but where and when do we go?

The alley behind the candy shop was empty of people, but many of the shop doors were open, allowing sounds and a few tantalizing smells to waft from within. The trio settled on the stairs to the little porch of the shop beside the candy shop. Henry handed out slightly-mangled sandwiches and the trio munched them in silence, lost in their thoughts once again.

"Okay," it was Henry who spoke first. "Nona, you can do this Glimpsing thing pretty well, right?"

Nona nodded, her mouth full of bread and sausage.

"So can you look at Winnie's farm, either right now or right after we left?"

Nona swallowed hard, wishing for a can of berry-flavored La Croix, her favorite soft drink, and wondering how many years had to pass until it would be invented. "I should be able to. Glimpsing isn't hard at all."

She sat up straight as an idea dawned on her. "You know, I didn't know that I could Glimpse until my family taught me how to do it. Maybe you two can Glimpse too and just don't know it yet."

Henry fell silent again, clearly lost in thought, for a few moments. Winnie looked at Nona with interest and, for the first time since the man at the river had grabbed her shoulders, stopped twisting around to look behind her every couple of minutes.

Henry broke the silence, sitting up straight with a purposeful look on his face. "I think I have a plan." He nodded several times as though agreeing with his own thoughts.

"I don't think we can stay here," Henry continued, gesturing broadly to everything around him with the squashed bag of food in his hand. He had set it on a crate when they arrived in the now-familiar alley behind Herr Hirschfield's shop, but had picked it right back up again when he saw something scurrying in the shadows. He hadn't set it back down since. "We know we can't go to the future and we think we can go back to Winnie's farm. Right?"

"We should be able to," Nona answered, looking at her companions and hoping with all her might that she was right. If not, they could each end up just about anywhere in history, alone and stranded. The thought of the three of them separated and experiencing anything like Henry's terrified arrival in the barn at Winnie's farm made her nauseous and dizzy. "I hope," she added.

Nona was looking toward the end of the alley with an intensity that made her companions turn and look in the same direction. When they saw nothing out of the ordinary, Henry asked, "What's wrong?"

"Hmm?" Nona looked around nervously. "What? What's wrong?"

"No. I was asking you what's wrong. You were a million miles away," Henry said, shaking his head and laughing.

"I've been thinking," he continued. "The best I can come up with is that we have to get someplace safe and figure out what each one of us can do – I mean Travel-wise. Then, maybe we can go back a little further and figure out how to fix things, or stop them from happening in the first place, or at least warn everyone who's going to be involved."

Nona wasn't sure it was a great plan, but she didn't have a better one. He was right, she thought, it *would* be good to know what abilities they each had. She looked at Winnie, who raised her eyebrows and shrugged. Clearly she didn't have a better plan either.

"The only problem with going back to Winnie's farm is timing." Nona said, frowning and thinking how crazy that sounded. She shook her head before continuing. "When my family was trying to tell me as much as they could about Travel, my Aunt Hildie said something about never coming into close proximity to myself in another time. I don't know what happens if you do meet yourself, but she sounded pretty serious about not doing it so I'm guessing it's not good."

"It seems to me that we aren't even supposed to be in terribly close proximity to our real-time selves for any length of time either," Nona's eyes were closed tightly as she tried to remember the flood of information that had come her way in the last couple of days in her own time. "I wonder if these things that aren't allowed are man-made rules or some sort of if-you-do-this-disaster-will-result warnings."

They all went silent for a bit, each wearing looks of great concern.

"Is there any place other than Winnie's farm you can think of where we will be safe while we figure things out?" Henry asked. The three sat in silence, frowning and eating their bread and keeping a watchful eye on the alley.

"Cliff Palace!" Nona blurted it out loudly enough to startle her friends. "The Wetherill brothers stumbled on it in 1888, sometime in December. That's a date that's in the past from where we are now. If we can just get there in the summer of that year, we will be able to find water and at least a little food for a day or two."

"I've been there!" Henry said, lighting up with excitement. "My family went to Mesa Verde on vacation when I was nine. We camped and I did the Junior Ranger classes." He delved into his seemingly bottomless stash of historical trivia, saying, "The Anasazi would have been long gone by the 1880s. The Indians that lived in the area thought the place was basically haunted and wouldn't go near it, and the ranchers didn't know it existed yet. Right?"

"Yeah," Nona answered, "although in my time, archeologists call the Anasazi 'Ancestral Puebloans' and American Indians are called 'Native Americans.'"

"What on earth are you talking about?" Winnie was looking peevish at being left out of the conversation. "Palaces? Cliffs?"

"In the southwest corner of Colorado, there are ruins of little cities that are tucked into caves on canyon walls. They were occupied by Native Americans, American Indians, hundreds of years ago, but then they were abandoned for reasons no one really understands. It's so dry out there, and they were so well built, that a lot of them are still standing and still in really good shape. In our times, they're part of a really beautiful National Park that gets lots and lots of visitors every summer, but if we go back before 1888, there should be no one there," Nona explained. The pristine air and long-abandoned cliff dwellings would be a welcome change, she thought, noticing an extremely well-fed rat scurrying along the opposite side of the little alley scaring up a host of plump, shiny cockroaches as he moved. Looking at Winnie, who had gone ashen, she knew she wasn't alone in spotting the rodent.

"Was Colorado a state in 1888?" Henry asked. Nona was about to tell him she didn't know, when Winnie chimed in.

"Of course it was," Winnie said, a little condescendingly. "It became the 38th state on August 1, 1876. What do people study in school in your times?"

"There's a lot more history to study by the time we get to school," Henry said, with a defensive edge in his voice.

Nona listened to her friends bicker about history for a few more moments before jumping in to settle things back down. "Henry's right," she said. "We can't stay here. Listen to yourselves – you're carrying on about nothing. We're all tired and scared. We have to get someplace quiet and safe and figure out what to do next. I vote for Cliff Palace in 1888."

"Me too," said Winnie, with wide, solemn eyes.

"Okay. Can you get us there?" Henry agreed.

Nona thought for a bit before answering. Her grandparents had taken her to Mesa Verde more times than she could count. The park was just down the road from Durango. The reason her grandparents had taken jobs at the college in Durango in the first place was its proximity to the hundreds of Anasazi ruins in southern Colorado. They had been involved in dozens of archeological digs over the years and had passed many of the stories of the great Anasazi civilization on to their granddaughter. Nona had hiked into various corners of the park with her anthropologist grandparents, seeing places that most visitors had no access to. She could remember seeing early photos of the cliff dwellings. Maybe concentrating on her memories of those photos would get them to the right era.

"I think I can," Nona said, trying to sound certain. "I'll Glimpse first and then we'll all go just like we did when we got here."

"Maybe we could ask Herr Hirschfield for a little more food and perhaps a little bottle of milk," Winnie suggested. "If we're careful with what he gives us, we will have a day or two to find food and drink on our own once we get there."

Nona was impressed with Winnie's practicality. She was beginning to understand the old saying that two heads were better than one, although in her case, it was three heads from three different times. Both Winnie and Henry had a different perspective on the world and seemed to think of things that didn't occur to her, or wouldn't have occurred to her until it was too late. It was easy to think of her two new friends as knowing less about the world than she did, since they both knew the world at an earlier time than she did. In reality, she thought, their knowledge of the world was proving to be a lot more useful than her own.

Henry crept up to the back of the candy shop and waited until it was empty of customers. He crept in and waved for the girls to follow him. Nona paused in the back hallway of the tiny shop and relished the intertwined smells of chocolates, taffies, mints and various candied fruits, all of which made a welcome change from the smells of filth and rot that filled the air of the alley. Henry explained to Mr. Hirschfield that they were going to leave the city and wondered if he could help them out with a little more food for their journey.

Herr Hirschfield was silent for a couple of minutes, staring at the children and their out-of-date, and for Nona and Henry ill-fitting, clothing with a worried look on his face. Finally, still frowning, he said, "Ja, you sree do not belong here. I can see zat. You vill go home now? Ja? You have money enough? Ja?"

"We will leave the city," Winnie said, speaking slowly and clearly weighing her words carefully. "It will take us a while to get home, but we will get there. We have everything we need for our Travels except food and a little milk." She had a relieved, satisfied look on her face as she finished.

The German candy maker looked satisfied by her words. He hurried about the shop, gathering some smoked sausages, dried fruits and an odd assortment of chocolates and candies, humming as he worked. Once he had a good-sized pile of food assembled, he rummaged in the back room for a few moments, emerging with two empty, cloth sugar sacks in his hand and a satisfied look on his face. He bundled the food into the sacks and spoke sternly about being careful and avoiding the docks. He directed his warnings to Henry, as though charging him with the girls' safety. The friends had just thanked him and promised to be careful when a woman in a maid's uniform came into the shop with a list in her hand. Henry caught Nona and Winnie's attention and gestured toward the back door with his head. The girls nodded. They said a quick goodbye to Herr Hirschfield and headed for the alley while Herr Hirschfield tended to his customer's list.

Back in the alley, the trio chose a spot on the enclosed porch of what looked liked an empty store a few doors down from the candy shop for the next step in their plan. Sitting close together, they positioned themselves so that Henry could keep watch and Winnie could keep an eye on Nona as she tried to concentrate on Glimpsing without distraction.

"Perhaps," Winnie said sort of tentatively, "we should hold onto you. It would be terrible if you were to disappear and we could never find each other again. If we're holding on to you, at least we would go with you."

"I think that's a good idea," Nona said, feeling the weight of responsibility for her companions. The girls positioned themselves so that Winnie could grip Nona's ankle with one hand and hold onto Henry's hand with the other.

Nona sat for several minutes, trying to clear her head, before attempting to Glimpse Mesa Verde. It took some real effort to chase all the stray thoughts out of her head. She realized that just thinking about her family brought her to the brink of tears. A few deep breaths later, she nodded to her friends and closed her eyes to get a Glimpse of Mesa Verde's Cliff Palace. It took only a moment for the soft beige color of the sleeping city to appear in her mind's eye. She took in the broad cave, its upper lip marked by dark streaks of mountain varnish and its bottom lip fringed by the upper branches of trees growing below the city. She was looking closely, trying to decide if she had hit the right era or not, when a Park Ranger walked along the front dwelling, checking corners as though preparing to lock up for the day. Nona sat up straight and popped her eyes open.

"Right place, wrong time," she said, frustrated by her failure. "I was looking at some time after it became a National Park."

"So you saw it the way you know it in your time?" Winnie asked.

"Pretty much, at least I think it was probably my time that I saw. I'm not sure how I'll know if I'm in the right time or not. The place hasn't changed much in hundreds of years, so I won't have any marker for what year it is."

"I don't know if Glimpsing works this way, but can you try to look at something else in the time you're trying to get to? Like maybe a town nearby, or the nearest big city. Maybe you can pin down the date that way and just sort of move your eyes to Mesa Verde? I don't know … " Henry was clearly as frustrated as she was.

Nona thought about it for a moment before saying, "I'm not sure, Henry, but it's the best idea we have at the moment. If I can Glimpse Durango during the summer of 1888, maybe you're right. Maybe I can just sort of shift west and a little south to Mesa Verde. It's worth a try."

Henry looked pleased with himself as he returned to sentry duty. Winnie asked if either of them needed anything, which they didn't, and then watched as Nona settled in for another Glimpse.

"You know, if you could spot a newspaper, perhaps you could find the date just as Henry did earlier," Winnie suggested timidly.

"Perfect," Nona said, sincerely. "I'll look for someone with a newspaper in Durango so I'll know the date. Thanks." Winnie responded with a big smile.

Nona closed her eyes again and took a few deep breaths as she thought about what her grandparents had told her about Durango in the late-19th century. She remembered that in the winter, when there was no tourism to speak of, some of the townspeople would close up their big, drafty houses and move into the old Strater Hotel, although the hotel would have been the new Strater Hotel then, or would it? Nona could picture it in her time, but wasn't certain of the year it was built. She did know that the town was growing in leaps in those years, the early, crude wooden structures being replaced by substantial brick buildings, many of which would still be standing in her own time.

Eventually an image began to form before her eyes. Muddy streets and wooden sidewalks came into focus. She could see women in fine dresses peering into shop windows. Women in plainer calico dresses peered as well, although staying back a bit from the better-dressed crowd and hanging onto the hands of children. Men in fancy suits strode along the sidewalks as if each was the mayor, tipping their hats to only the best-dressed women. Men in chaps, cowboy boots and sweat-stained cowboy hats loped along, stepping aside for the women, children and well-dressed men alike. The cowboys tipped their hats to every woman they passed.

Nona gasped at the colors, causing Winnie to tighten her grip. All the photos she had seen of old Durango were in black and white, as were all photos from the late 1800s. The women's fine dresses were all done in deep, rich colors with lots of trim. The calicos were brighter, but still in rich reds, blues and greens. The girl's dresses were done in much lighter, pretty pastel shades. The hats worn by the women in fancy clothing were astounding creations. They were the size of the platter her mother used for the Thanksgiving turkey, some even bigger, Nona thought, and they were piled high with netting, fringes, silk flowers and fake birds with real feathers. The women wore their hair pulled up and puffed out somehow, making the hats look as though they were riding on a great cloud of hair. Men in dark suits strutted down the streets, swinging walking sticks with definite swaggers. Men in loose-fitting denim trousers and huge cowboy hats tethered their dusty horses to hitching posts. Nona reached out with her mind, as though wandering along the street, looking at the business names painted ornately on the false fronts of the buildings as she went. She spotted a dry goods store, something called an assayer, and a yard goods store.

Nona saw the outline of the towering San Juan mountains ahead of her, which gave her bearings in a city she would know so well in more than 100 years. She turned to look down the street for the old Strater Hotel building, where she had enjoyed lunch with her grandparents just a few days earlier, although in her own time. When she spotted it, she froze – the old Strater was there and it was brand new. It towered above the other buildings on the street, looking somehow much bigger than it would in a time when it was surrounded by newer buildings. She moved toward it in her mind and saw a nicely dressed man sitting on a bench beside the ornate front door of the hotel. He was holding up a newspaper, but looking over the top of it at a man struggling to control the horses pulling his wagon through town. Working hard to focus her mind, she zeroed in on the paper in his hands and frowned as she tried to make out the date. June 3, 1888. She grinned at the discovery.

Keeping her eyes closed and speaking softly and slowly so as not to disturb the image, she told Winnie and Henry, "I'm in Durango on the third of June in 1888." Neither one responded, but she knew they had heard her and was sure they were just trying not to disturb her Glimpse. Nona tried to pull herself back from the image, as though trying to get an overhead view of the city. She realized she was tilting her head from side to side and thought it must look odd to her friends. The thought made the image blur a bit, startling her into concentrating again. The image cleared up and she went on trying to pull back and redirect her efforts to the southwest.

Rising high above Durango for a better vantage point, Nona saw the broad, flat Montezuma Valley stretching off toward the west and the reclining form of the mountain range known as Sleeping Ute in the far distance. She followed the path she knew the highway would take at some point in the future, eventually spotting Point Lookout, the high, proud tip of the mesa system that would someday make up the park.

Although she had been in the park dozens of times, the landscape looked completely foreign to her without the long, winding roads that connected the mesa tops and canyon bottoms, and without the cozy enclave of park buildings at Morefield Campground and up at Far View. It took a few Glimpses into the wrong canyons before she finally spotted Cliff Palace off in the distance. She realized that she wouldn't have spotted it at all had she not known exactly what to look for, and envied Wetherill his first thrilling sight of the sleeping city. In just six months, she thought with wonder, he would be riding these mesas and canyons looking for stray cattle and would find a lost civilization. She moved closer to the cliff dwelling that once housed more than 400 people, looking closely for any signs of human presence. A golden eagle drifted overhead, a few ravens clucked from their perches in the trees, but other than a few birds, there was no sign of activity.

"I've got it," Nona said softly, keeping her eyes closed and mental gaze fixed on the cliff dwelling as she pulled the pouches out of her dress and raised her elbows toward her companions. "Take out your pouches and then hold on tight to my arms. We should be good to go."

Henry took one last look up and down the alley before moving toward Nona and Winnie. A quivering Winnie pressed close to Nona's left side, hooking her arm in her friend's. She closed her eyes and tried to take deep, relaxed breaths. Henry sat down at Nona's right side and hooked his arm in hers too.

"Take my hands too," Nona said, not daring to move lest she lose sight of the dwelling. She felt her friends grip her hands, their arms entwined with hers and their shoulders pressed tightly against her own, and took the plunge into the past. The dizzying sensations of Travel that had terrified her just a few days earlier now seemed reassuring. She was Traveling and she could feel her two friends on her arms as time raced by.

Elaine Schmidt

CHAPTER 13

Had anyone been watching the cliff dwelling at that moment on June 3, 1888, they would have been stunned to see three children appear out of thin air and plop, in a sprawling tangle of arms and legs, onto the lip of the cave that housed the largest of the Mesa Verde cliff dwellings. But no one was watching. The dwellings, in fact the entire system of deep, dramatic canyons, had been abandoned for centuries. The Navajo and Ute peoples knew of the dwellings but avoided them out of fear and respect for the spirits they believed haunted them.

The children had dropped into the last months of isolation and silence the canyons would know. Historians, photographers and plunderers would begin arriving in the canyons within the year. Wetherill's accidental discovery would begin a series of archeological digs and studies that would continue into Nona's time. The history of the cliff dwellers, who were known for many years as Anasazi, the Navajo word for Ancient Enemies, and later as Ancestral Puebloans, would become part of the story of America. The constant human traffic in those early years, followed by hordes of park visitors, would take a tremendous toll on both the delicate, arid ecosystem and on the fragile ruins tucked into the canyon walls and scattered on the mesa tops. But in the moment of the children's arrival, the canyons were silent and empty, having sat largely untouched by humans since the builders of the dwellings had disappeared mysteriously centuries earlier.

Nona was stunned to see the towers and structures of Cliff Palace crumbling to rubble. She dimly remembered her grandparents telling her that the cliff dwellings had been rebuilt and stabilized before tourists were allowed through them, but the sight of a nearly ruined Cliff Palace was still shocking.

Henry was the first to get his bearings after the trio's arrival. He glanced at his companions, who were trying to disentangle their arms, legs and skirts and checking for scrapes and other injuries. He rose unsteadily to his feet and began to take in their new surroundings. He spun slowly, his eyes darting left to right and up and down, making two complete revolutions before dropping to his knees beside the girls.

"I think we're alone," he whispered. "Are you two alright?" Both girls nodded, Nona quickly glancing around to take in the reality of where they were, Winnie looking pale and staring at Cliff Palace with her mouth hanging open.

"Let's get out of sight anyway," Henry said, clearly nervous about being out in the open in a strange place and time. He looked at Nona with eyebrows raised and she stood and took the lead.

"In my time, the rangers warn everyone to stay off the edges of walls and not to disturb anything," she said, gently picking her way into the interior of the cliff dwelling. "I guess we should try to do the same so that we don't disturb the site any more than we have to." In the next second, Winnie stumbled and nearly took a bad fall. Henry and Nona both reached out and caught her arms, steadying her.

"I'm sorry," she cried. "I just can't stop looking at these buildings. Tell me again who lived here and what happened to them."

"How about if we talk when we've found a spot to settle in for a while," Henry said, in a stage whisper. Carrying the sacks of food, he poked his head into the doorway of a tall, tower-like structure. "I think this will do." He gestured to the lower level of the tower.

Looking into the tower room, Nona noticed that the sandy floor showed no signs of water, either dripping or collecting in puddles. Winnie stuck her head through the opening and pointed out that there were no signs of animals having been in the space either. The three children shared a look and nodded in unison. They had found a safe haven, at least for the time being.

Nona entered the dusty little room with the intention of working out some of the group's problems. She agreed with Henry that they needed to find out what Travel abilities each of them possessed. She also knew they had to come up with a plan to sort out what was happening in her time and why it had apparently set someone on their trail. The state of her grandparents' house, that she didn't know what had happened there and that she hadn't heard a word from her family were all nagging at her. She was afraid to mention her concerns about Winnie's family for fear of upsetting her friend, but there had clearly been Travelers heading toward the farm when she had fled with Winnie and Henry grabbing on and tagging along. But her worries dimmed as the three Travelers settled into comfortable positions in the dark, cool interior of the ancient room. Nona realized that it had been several days since she had had the luxury of sleeping through a night. She looked at her friends as they slumped against the rough, painted surface of the small room's adobe walls and saw the same exhaustion in their faces. She was about to suggest that they sleep for a bit, when Henry succumbed to an enormous yawn.

"Do you think we can try and sleep a little?" he asked shaking his head as though he was fighting to stay awake.

"I don't think we will have to try very hard," Winnie added, catching the yawn from Henry. Nona pulled off her two petticoats, much to Winnie's horror, and handed one to Henry. She told Winnie to pull off one of her own and explained that the desert air would get chilly when the sun went down. The petticoats were the closest things to blankets they had on hand. Winnie made Henry close his eyes before she stood, turned her back to him, unfastened one of her petticoats and let it drop to the ground, blushing madly the entire time.

Once they were all settled under their makeshift blankets, Winnie dissolved into gentle rhythmic snoring in a matter of minutes. Henry commented that it was beginning to get dark outside. He said that since it was June in the southwest, it must be about nine in the evening. Nona was trying to calm the jumble of thoughts racing through her head when Henry spoke again.

"Nona, are you awake?"

"Mostly."

"Do you really think we are going to be able to figure out what's going on in your time?"

"I do," she said, with more assurance than she felt. "We have to. It's the only way any of us are going to get home. Let's try and sleep and we'll get to work in the morning."

He glanced at Winnie, who was fast asleep, before continuing. "I'm worried about Winnie's folks. We don't know what happened back there."

"Me too," Nona said through an enormous yawn. The two sat in silence a moment, both fighting falling asleep.

"Should one of us stay awake?" he asked, sounding a bit nervous. "Should we stand watch?"

Nona thought about the question a moment before answering. "No. I think we're safe here." She hoped she was right. There was almost no chance of running into people in the canyons at this point in history, but there were other things to be aware of. Snakes would be the biggest concern, but since there were no signs of animals in the room they had chosen, Nona decided to believe that there was little chance of snakes hanging around either. "I think we can just go to sleep."

And sleep they did. When Nona next opened her eyes there was a bright shaft of sunlight streaming into the little room. The clucking of a raven from somewhere nearby was the only sound Nona could hear. She sat up, feeling an unfamiliar stiffness from the unusual experience of sleeping on a dirt floor in a desert cliff dwelling. Nona looked around to see if her companions were still sleeping. She was surprised to find herself alone in the little room. Scrambling to her knees, she popped her head through the keyhole-shaped doorway and was instantly blinded by bright sunlight.

She pulled her head back into the shadows of the room and waited for a few moments with her eyes closed before squinting toward the doorway again. As her eyes began to adjust to the brightness, she slowly made her way out of the room to find her friends. Still squinting, Nona spotted Winnie on the far side of the cliff dwelling, sitting neatly on the lip of the cave that housed the ancient city. Winnie was looking out at the pristine canyon with a look of utter wonder on her face.

"Good morning," Nona called to her. Winnie turned to wave at Nona before getting to her feet and making her way carefully across the rubble to Nona.

"This place is truly amazing," Winnie said, her eyes shining with excitement. "On the exterior walls of the buildings, you can see how they were made with big stones and mortar and then little stones shoved in the mortar. A lot of the rooms have beautiful designs painted on the walls. I almost expect people to come up the path and ask me why I'm peeking into their houses. And the canyon is so beautiful I can hardly believe it, and everything smells so good compared to where we were."

Nona smiled, remembering her first sight of the cliff dwellings. The sleeping cities, neatly tucked in caves, with their tidily chinked walls really were marvels. All of them faced south, where sunlight warmed them in the winter and shadows from the cliffs above cooled them in the summer. Each collection of buildings was uniquely fitted to contours of the caves – some tall and elegant, like Tower House, and some short and broad, like Spruce Tree House. The caves tended to echo, which always made Nona wonder what they must have sounded like centuries ago when they were filled with families performing the noisy business of daily life.

"I know," Nona said looking around. "I've spent, or I guess I will spend, a lot of time here with my grandparents, and it still amazes me whenever I see it. The canyon looks about the same in my time as it does now, but a lot of the cliff dwellings have been rebuilt and there are some trails and stairs outside the dwellings to keep visitors safe. There are almost always visitors, and a lot of them. Even so, the place kind of makes me want to whisper, although I don't know why." Both girls looked around them in silence for a few moments.

"Where's Henry?" Nona asked, a little concerned by the silence and thought of the trio getting separated in the vastness of the canyons.

"He said he was going to reconnoiter the area, which apparently means to survey it in some fashion," Winnie said, gesturing toward the huge canyon system with a little frown. "He's been gone quite a long while now."

Nona walked to the edge of the cave, cupped her hands around her mouth and yelled Henry's name at the top of her lungs. The only sounds that came back to her were her own echo and a few irritated squawks from ravens. She cupped her hands around her mouth again, but this time she took a deep breath and let out a piercing whistle. Within a couple of seconds, two short whistles came back to her from somewhere below the cave and off to the left.

It took Henry about a half hour to make his way back through the thick undergrowth of the canyon bottom and up the treacherous trails on the canyon wall, but when he arrived, he proved worth the wait. He had made a hammock out of his shirttail and had filled it with what looked to Nona like the contents of a Thanksgiving cornucopia.

"There's a river down there that's just bursting with fish," Henry said, grinning and panting heavily from scrambling up the last few yards of the ancient trail leading to the cliff dwelling. "I nearly caught some with my bare hands. It's just incredible down there – like the Garden of Eden." With that he dumped the contents of his shirt onto the ground, creating a mound of pine nuts, dried-up serviceberries, yucca roots and a couple of dried ears of corn. He sat down beside Winnie, with a loud "whew" of exhaustion.

"Aren't you the Boy Scout!" Nona was laughing at Henry's wet trouser legs, muddy shoes and the burrs still clinging to his clothing and hair.

"I am, actually, and I'm proud of it," he said, sounding a little defensive. "When I got up this morning and started really looking around, I realized this place is not that far from Philmont, or at least from where Philmont will be. I spent two weeks at the camp last summer. We had to take survival classes. I started thinking about the things we were taught to look for and I thought maybe this place would have some of the same stuff we gathered there. It does."

"What's a boy scout and what's a philmont?" Winnie said, with an irritated edge in her voice. "I'm growing weary of not knowing what you two are talking about."

"That's right," Henry said with a faraway look on his face. "The Boy Scouts won't exist until 1910. And Philmont was pretty new when my dad went there as a Scout." He turned to face Winnie and sat down beside her. "I'm sorry, Winnie. It's really hard for me to remember that you come from such a different time. I've seen your time and I know you're part of it, but it's hard for me to remember that. You're my friend, not part of a different century."

Winnie gave him a warm smile. "I know what you mean. I try to imagine what your worlds must be like and I can't begin to picture how spectacular they must be. You know about so many things that haven't happened and haven't been invented in my time. Well, sometimes I feel like you two are an awful lot smarter than I am."

"Are you kidding? I feel the same way about you," Nona said, sitting down with them. "You know how to cook and sew and know how to help when a calf is born and other things that I have no idea about. Somehow you seem a lot more grown up than kids in my time."

"Okay, new rule," Henry said, picking burrs from his pant legs. "We all have to feel free to ask about things we don't understand from the others' times and we can't let ourselves feel like we don't know things we should know. I mean, a week ago we couldn't have imagined we would be sitting here in this now and talking to people from other times. So we just have to get used to it and stick together. Right?"

"Right," the girls said, almost in unison. They looked at each other, giggled and added, "In this now?"

"Hey, don't laugh," Henry said, laughing himself. "The lingo of all this Travel stuff is tough. But what's more important," he said, waving the two ears of corn at Nona and Winnie, "is how do we cook this stuff?"

Winnie took the helm, after muttering the word "lingo" a few times, and explained that the berries should be soaked in water for a while so they would soften up, the corn should be soaked too, but then it would have to be cooked. The pine nuts were edible raw, but they would taste better if they were roasted.

"I can get a fire started," Henry said, sounding proud of this skill. "Oh, Winnie, Boy Scouts are an organization designed to teach leadership and skills to boys. There are a bunch of levels for different ages. You earn badges, do service projects, camp and other stuff. Philmont is a big camp in New Mexico for Boy Scouts from all over the country."

"Thank you, Henry," Winnie said, with a proper nod of her head. "What's new Mexico?"

Nona and Henry stared at her for a moment before Nona said, "I guess it wasn't a state yet in your time. I never realized how little I knew about the history of the various states."

"No matter," Winnie said, standing up and brushing the dust off her skirts. "Henry, I can help you gather kindling and wood for the fire. Nona, I looked in the doorway of that building earlier," with which she pointed to one of the buildings near the tower. "I saw a pot that looked like it had been sat on quite a few fires. We can use that for water. Henry, is it terribly far to the river?"

"We don't need the river," Nona said, remembering her grandmother's many lectures on the wonders of Anasazi culture. "There are seep springs at the backs of all of these caves. Rainwater is filtered as it passes through the sandstone, so it's clean enough to drink without boiling it first."

Smiling, the three Travelers set to their tasks with purpose. Henry helped Winnie navigate the trail down to the trees below the dwelling, while Nona went to retrieve the pot. She couldn't help but think of her grandparents and how horrified they would be at the thought of their granddaughter disturbing an archeological artifact, let alone filling it up with water and cooking with it. She located the pot where Winnie had said it would be. After a pause to say "Sorry about this" to the past and the future, she picked it up and made her way around to the back of the cave where a fresh, moist smell in the otherwise dusty air led her to the seep spring.

When they had all returned to the edge of the cave, Winnie pointed to one of the round rooms that reached deep into the floor of the cave and asked, "Why are some of the houses square and some round? And for that matter, why are some tall and some sunken like that?"

"The taller structures are the actual houses," Nona said, realizing as she spoke that she sounded an awful lot like her grandmother teaching a class. "The round rooms in the ground are kivas, which were ceremonial spaces. The people who lived here believed their ancestors came into this world from a world below it. I think that's why the kivas are sunken into the ground."

The Travelers stopped to look at the circular shapes of the kivas sunken around them. Standing still, they each wandered off into their own thoughts for a few moments, adding to the silence of the rambling canyon. As if on cue, they turned to look at each other and went back to their tasks.

Building the fire, soaking the berries and corn and roasting the pine nuts took the better part of two hours. When Henry saw Winnie sniffing and pinching the yucca roots with an uncertain look on her face, he offered an explanation.

"That's a yucca root," he said, picking that moment to work on removing the burrs in his hair. "It's a great soap."

"It's also a great shampoo," Nona added. "It's as though it has conditioner built into it. It makes your hair really shiny."

"Conditioner?" Winnie was frowning.

"The stuff you put on your hair after you shampoo it," Nona said, realizing she hadn't been at Winnie's house long enough to take a complete bath and wash her hair.

"We use vinegar to rinse out the soap," Winnie said, pausing to watch Henry try to disentangle burrs from his seriously untidy mop of hair. Nona had to giggle, thinking that their present dirty, disheveled state was a pretty poor commercial for hygiene products. Winnie caught her eye and shared the giggle.

Once the food was ready, the Travelers feasted on Henry's gatherings and some of Herr Hirschfield's bread, saving the sausage, candied fruits and other sweets he had included for later. When they were done, they lounged in the shade for a bit, enjoying their full stomachs and the peaceful surroundings. The girls were just beginning to doze when Henry startled them awake.

"Look! Quick!" he said in excited whisper, pointing at the sky. Soaring high above the canyon was an enormous golden eagle. It sailed across their field of vision, tilting slightly to catch the air, but never once flapping its wings. They watched in silence until it had passed.

Wide awake from the excitement of the eagle sighting, the three friends turned to look at each other. Nona knew they were all thinking the same thing, so she put it into words. "We have to make a plan. We can't just hang out here forever," she said. Her friends nodded in agreement, Winnie quietly repeating "hang out" a few times, as though trying it on for size.

"We need to know what abilities we have as Travelers," she continued.

"What makes you think I have any at all?" Winnie said, with a note of worry in her voice. "All I've managed to do is have some odd dreams and grab hold of you and trail along."

"My grandfather told me that people can either Travel or they can't. Levels of abilities vary quite widely, but most people can't move through time or Glimpse or even dream about other times at all. I think the fact that you could Travel with us must mean that you have some abilities. He also said that abilities usually appear at about our ages. He said that you can learn a lot and develop a lot of abilities in your first few years of Travel, but then most people sort of level off and don't gain many more abilities."

Winnie's face brightened considerably. "So I must be a Traveler too!"

"I think so." It dawned on Nona that Winnie had been feeling sort of left out, thinking she was just being dragged along like baggage. She resolved to pay more attention to what her friends were feeling, regretting that she had been so consumed by her own worries the past few days.

"Maybe a good place to start would be figuring out if we can Glimpse like you can," Henry suggested.

The girls agreed that this sounded like a reasonable starting point. Nona explained the process as her family had explained it to her, adding several descriptions about the sensation of Glimpsing that her family, who took Glimpsing and Traveling pretty much for granted after decades of doing it, hadn't provided. She suggested that they make another set of homing pouches, feeling a bit angry with herself for not thinking of this when they first arrived. What if Henry had disappeared? How would they ever have found him?

They sacrificed a little more of her petticoat, which she was delighted to be getting rid of anyway, to create three pouches with pebbles from Cliff Palace and a few newly-opened flowers as anchors to that place on that very morning. They all stowed their previous pouches in their pockets, agreeing that they had better have them handy at all times in case they needed them. Henry suggested covering them with rocks so that nothing could sniff them out and eat them, which sounded like a good idea to the girls. The trio stopped at the seep spring for a sip of cool water before sitting down in a cool, shaded recess of the huge cave to work on Glimpsing.

Nona took the first turn, whispering explanations about what she was thinking and imagining as she concentrated on Glimpsing her grandparents' house. When her vision began to cloud and details of her grandparents' dining room began to appear, she fell silent and concentrated on what she was seeing. The house was still in complete disarray. She turned her head and looked around the rooms in the main part of the house. She couldn't see anything that was different from her quick Visit a few days earlier. Taking a look into the hallway, she moved her concentration upstairs to the room where she slept, gasping quietly at what she saw. On the foot of her bed lay a neatly-folded quilt that was both familiar and unfamiliar. It looked a lot like Winnie's quilt, or at least the fabrics did. But the pattern was completely different and the quilt looked as though it had seen some hard use over the years. She stared at it for a moment before returning her attention to her companions, where she was greeted by twin expressions of fear and concern.

"What did you see?" Henry's voice was tense.

"Someone must have been at the house," Nona said, frowning as she tried to think what the quilt might mean. "There was a quilt sitting on the edge of my bed. It was made of the same fabric as Winnie's quilt, but it was different, a different pattern entirely."

"That must have been my mother's quilt," Winnie said, with a far away sound in her voice. "Her mother gave her fabric for a quilt when she was about 16. She didn't use it all up in the pattern she chose, so she put it away to save for another quilt. She brought it out last winter, when we were snowed in for several weeks, and she let me use it for a quilt."

"Do you think it means something that someone left it there? Like maybe it's some kind of message?" Henry asked.

"I think it was a message, but I'm not sure what the message was." Nona fell silent and stewed about the quilt and its possible meaning, while the others watched her.

After a few minutes Henry suggested that they continue their project of sorting out their own abilities for the time being and think about the quilt later.

Henry took the next turn at Glimpsing, deciding to focus on his own time and his family. Nona coached him, reminding him that no one would be able to see him, until an astonished look came across his face.

He whispered something that sounded like "I see it" before his expression changed to one of deep sadness. Whatever he saw, he watched it for several minutes with a grim expression before returning his attention to the girls.

"My parents don't know where I am," he said with a heavy, flat sound in his voice. "The police are at the house, dusting things for fingerprints and looking for footprints in the yard. They think I was kidnapped."

"Oh Henry, I'm sorry," Nona said. She couldn't imagine how she would feel if she thought her parents didn't know what had happened to her. That thought made her realize that while her parents knew she was Traveling, they really had no idea what had happened to her in the past few days or where and when she had landed.

CHAPTER 14

"What's a fingerprint?" Winnie managed to break the sour mood.

"What?" Henry stared at her.

"What is a fingerprint and what's this about dust?"

"Wait a minute," Nona said, getting up and hurrying off to find a good-sized potshard she had noticed earlier, thinking at the time that her grandparents would have loved to see it. It was made of long, narrow ropes of clay, each one pressed onto the one below and pinched into little peaks and valleys by someone's fingertips. She knew from her grandmother's stories that the interior of the pot had been smoothed, probably with a rounded stone, before it was placed in a pit and fired for strength. The crimping on the outside of the pot still showed the perfectly preserved fingerprints of the person who had made it hundreds of years earlier.

"See those tiny fine patterns of lines in the clay?" she asked Winnie, pointing to the little pinched-up peaks. Winnie leaned in and looked closely before nodding. "Those are fingerprints that were left there by the person who made the pots centuries ago. Every person on the planet has a different pattern of lines and grooves on their fingertips. When a person touches things, at least some things, they leave a print of that line-and-groove pattern behind. Sometime around the turn of the century, not so far from your time, scientists will figure that out and police will begin using fingerprints left at crime scenes as evidence to identify criminals. A special, fine powder is used to make the prints more visible."

Winnie was examining her own fingertips and comparing them to Nona's with a look of wonder on her face. Henry, at least temporarily distracted from his worries about his parents, was taking a close look at the prints on the pot. Nona thought briefly about the fact that her family's instructions to avoid revealing things about the future had pretty much gone out the window and wondered if she could even begin to make Winnie understand the idea of DNA testing. That led her to wonder if Henry knew about DNA testing. She let the distraction of the fingerprints play itself out before suggesting that Winnie try to Glimpse her home.

Winnie listened to Nona's coaching and squinted as she attempted to see her home. She became rather red-faced with the effort before her eyes popped wide open and she blurted, "It's no use," in a frustrated, disappointed voice.

"Maybe you're trying too hard," Henry suggested, with a thoughtful sound in his voice. "For me it felt like I just had to let go and imagine my house and my family and then I could see them as clear as day."

Winnie rubbed her eyes, sighed deeply, straightened her skirt and then announced she would try again. This time she stared off at the back of the cave with a glassy look in her eyes for a few moments. Eventually, her eyes closed, but her face remained calm. After a minute or two her spine stiffened and her expression changed to one of wonder. "There you are," she whispered. A second later, she turned to Nona with her eyes shining. "I could see you and me. It was the day you popped into my bedroom for a few seconds. We both looked awfully surprised." Her voice was nothing less than triumphant.

Nona listened, tickled by Winnie's obvious delight in her newly discovered ability. But she had more on her mind than Winnie's success. She had stopped listening to Winnie's excited descriptions of what she had just seen, retreating into her own thoughts and worries.

"You know," she said, hating to interrupt Winnie, but getting antsy to get moving. "I'm sorry, but I think it's time for me to get a really good look at that quilt. I'm sure it leads to some place and time that will hold some answers as to what's going on and what happened to my family."

Nona paused and let her friends catch up with her thoughts before adding, "I think I need to go back to my time for a little while and see if I can figure out what that old quilt means."

Winnie's face went immediately white with a look of complete horror. Henry's reaction was less dramatic, but Nona could see that he was worried too.

"I don't like the sound of us getting separated one bit," Winnie said, in a shrill voice, shaking her head as though punctuating her statement. "I believe that's the worst possible idea."

Henry was shaking his head and frowning and muttering "what if" softly to himself.

"I'm open to other ideas," Nona said feeling oddly defensive, "I just don't happen to have any."

"What if you Glimpsed your grandparents' house in your time and tried to focus on the quilt that was left out for you. Do you think you could go from there to Glimpse it in its time?"

Nona and Winnie just stared at Henry.

"I was just thinking," he said quickly, with bright eyes. "Your family knows by now that we're all together, don't you think? I mean, they're in our future and we're in their past. They at least know you're with Winnie because they sent you to her. So if they wanted to get us a message or send us somewhere, they wouldn't do it in a way that would risk separating us, or at least you and Winnie, would they?"

Winnie and Nona both had looks of dawning understanding. Clearly encouraged, Henry went on, saying, "I think they would send you someplace we could all go together, which would have to be in all of our pasts. Right? At least that's what I would do."

"I think you have a point," Nona said. "They would also have a pretty good idea of what I would be able to do, even if I don't know myself. I mean, maybe Glimpsing within a Glimpse is really simple to do. I just don't know that because I've never tried it."

Winnie, whose face had regained some color, said calmly, "If you can describe to me what you're seeing when you try to Glimpse the older quilt, I can try to tell you if it sounds right. My Aunt Mary lives in the house my grandparents built and I've been there several times. I think it should look very much like I know it in my time."

"We all down with that?" Nona asked.

"What?" Henry and Winnie responded in perfect unison with matching looks of confusion on their faces.

"With my trying to … " Nona stopped, realizing they understood the plan perfectly, they didn't understand the "down with that" part of the question. "Do we have a plan then?"

Henry and Winnie agreed that they had a plan.

"Perhaps we should all clasp hands as you Glimpse," Winnie said with a practical tone in her voice. "Since we can't go to the future, maybe our holding on to you will keep you in place here while you're looking at the future. If we chance to go with you to the time of the older quilt, at least we would all be together." The three friends looked at each other with worried faces, nodding in silent agreement.

They headed back to their little room, after agreeing that they all felt better out of sight even though they knew there was no one around for many miles to see them. Nona took a last look out at the canyon and up at the mesa top, before stepping into the room. She thought that perhaps one of the Native Americans had seen them arrive, or perhaps depart. That could be the root of the ghost stories about the place that were still being told in her own time, or at least a chapter in the stories. Thinking about causing something that she would hear about in more than a century made her a little dizzy.

They used the two petticoats that were still on the floor, Winnie having apparently put hers back on before stepping out that morning, as cushions to sit on, and arranged themselves as though gathering around a very small campfire. Both Winnie and Henry held one of Nona's arms with both of their hands, clearly worried about her slipping into the future or past without them. Nona closed her eyes and tried to Glimpse the old quilt in her grandparents' house.

"I see the quilt at my grandparents' house," Nona whispered, after a couple of minutes of quiet concentration. She frowned as she concentrated on the quilt, before taking a few slow, deep breaths in an attempt to relax. As the frown left her face, she uttered a soft, "Oh!"

Winnie and Henry held a little tighter as Nona said, "Winnie, I see a small house, with a really low ceiling. The walls are kind of wavy. They have wallpaper on them, but they sort of bulge in spots – it's hard to describe."

"No, you have got it just right," Winnie whispered back. "It's a soddy. A few rooms of the house were built of bricks of dirt. It got a little out of plumb over the years, so the walls are definitely wavy. The ceilings are low enough that everyone has to duck in parts of the house. There are wooden planks in the ceilings, so if you bump your head, you'll remember it."

Nona's eyes popped open, the image disappeared and she grinned at her friends, saying, "I've got it!"

"What's the message?" Henry asked, his voice loud with excitement.

"What message?" Nona looked confused for a moment before adding, "Oh, the quilt. No, not that. I've been thinking that before we leave here to find the older quilt, or go anywhere else, we have to come up with a way to get our hands on some money. I've been worried about us wandering through time without a penny between us, just hoping to run into some nice candy inventor who will feed us. It just occurred to me that I know exactly how to do it."

Winnie and Henry shared a worried look.

"No, no, nothing illegal or anything," Nona said, with a laugh. "When I was little I was riding my scooter in my grandparents' house on a rainy day. I knew I shouldn't, but I was really bored with being indoors. Anyways, I hit the baseboard with it and a piece of wood popped off. I tried to put it back as quickly as I could, which is when I found a metal box tucked in the opening. Of course, I opened it. Inside there was all kinds of money from different countries and different times. Some of it quite old and most of it really beautiful."

"What was it doing there?" Henry asked.

"Well, my grandmother found me looking at it and she said that it had been there when they bought the house and they thought it was fun to just leave it there as a reminder of the long history of the old house," Nona had a look on her face as though she had just found an answer she had been searching for. "But knowing that they're Travelers, I'll bet it was there in case they needed cash from different times and places for their Travels. I mean, it's not like you can go to the bank in 2011 and say you need $500 in French money from 1750 for a trip you're taking."

"Ooh, I would wager you're right," Winnie said, clearly enjoying solving a mystery. "But you can't go back there, so what good does it do us?"

"I have an idea," Nona said, trying to ignore the dubious looks on her friends' faces. "I'll Glimpse first and then go back to just before Henry Traveled to see if the box is there. They've lived in that house since 1972 – right by the front door is a framed photo of them on the day they moved in and the date is written on it. Henry, you Glimpse while I go, and keep a lookout for me, just in case something goes wrong. Winnie you hold on to him to make sure he doesn't accidentally Travel."

Henry and Winnie both started to object, but neither one uttered a complete sentence before falling silent.

"I know, I don't really like it either," Nona said. "But we are going to need some money if we intend to eat once we leave Mesa Verde."

Henry looked as though he was doing math in his head. "You should probably take any currency you find that dates to Winnie's time or before. We can't very well pull out a 1950s bill in her time or any earlier," he said. "But I don't know what I'm trying to Glimpse, so how am I going to find it?"

They all fell silent contemplating this latest wrinkle, until Nona said, "How about if both of you try something with me. We are in June of 1888, so the Strater Hotel is almost brand new in Durango, which is just down the road." Nona paused to get her directions straight, before saying "that way" and pointing over her shoulder.

"You should be able to find the hotel with no trouble," she continued. "It's a big, fancy brick place that should be bustling with activity. It will look really out of place with what stands around it. Once you see it, I can give you directions to their house, because it's only a few blocks away. The house should be there in this time and it should be quite new."

Nona paused to think through what she thought the next step should be. Speaking more slowly, she went on, "From there we can just work forward to the right time. It may take a while, but I think it will work. It's similar to the way I got us here. Winnie, I'm not entirely certain how this works yet, but I'm sure you won't be able to Glimpse the future any more than you'd be able to Travel there, so you may have to drop out at that point. Henry, you stay with me and we'll just move forward until we find a time just after they bought the house. Then you can keep Glimpsing as a lookout and I'll Travel and grab some of the cash."

Henry was nodding and looking pretty eager, but Winnie had a grim look on her face.

"Nona, isn't this stealing?" she asked gravely.

"I thought about that too, but I don't think it is," Nona said. "That money has to be there for Travels. Why else would they keep it tucked away like that? They would care a lot more about us being safe and fed than about that money. I'll leave a note and they'll know exactly what happened. It may even help them find us."

Now it was Henry's turn to look worried. He shook his head in disagreement before saying, "I'm sure you're right about the money, but I think you have to be careful about what you say in the note. You want to tell your family where you are, but not anyone else who might stumble on the note."

"Oh yes," Winnie agreed, clearly over her worries about whether or not they were stealing. "You are going to have to be careful and cryptic."

"Good point," Nona said. "Maybe we should figure out what I should write before we try this. I may have to hurry once I'm there."

The friends tried several different messages, each one more complex than the last before agreeing that simplicity was the best option. In the end, they decided that a simple "Got your message, went back to check it out" would do the trick.

"Perhaps you should capitalize the B in 'back,'" Winnie suggested as they settled to put their plan into action. "That should let them know that you mean backwards in time, not just back to their house."

Nona responded with a nod, warned Henry to stay with her and ask questions if he started to get lost, before taking a deep breath and saying, "Let's get started."

The trio closed their eyes and began the process of relaxing and imagining that led to Glimpsing. Nona guided them above and away from the canyons, the sight of which made Winnie gasp and reminded Nona that she would never have seen anything from such a height, having never flown or even imagined an airplane or a skyscraper yet. She forced her attention back to the task at hand and guided her friends to Durango, where the Strater Hotel loomed over what looked more like a muddy cow town than the hopping resort area it would one day become.

"How grand," Winnie whispered.

"Look at all the cowboys," Henry chimed in quietly.

"Okay," Nona said, make sure you're facing the mountains and then turn to your right and start moving slowly in that direction. You're looking for a neighborhood of big brick and stone houses. Once you find it, look for a red brick house with a large, horse-shoe-shaped window facing the street."

There was silence as Henry and Winnie tried to control the direction their minds took, but they both finally cried out that they saw it.

"Good," Nona said, trying to keep her voice calm. "Let's try moving forward. Henry, maybe it would work for you to try imagining the seasons turning, or imagining the house with people, or cars, or something else from later eras. I don't know."

Anyone looking at the little trio, huddled alone in the vastness of Colorado's canyon country with their eyes closed and their minds far away, would have thought they had been hypnotized or drugged. They were all sitting as still as statues, Henry and Winnie hanging on to each other's arms, breathing deeply and slowly as they let their minds do the work of transporting them through time.

"Christmases," Henry said quietly, "I can see the Christmases go by."

Nona tried to do the same and found that he was right. It looked as though the house was sitting empty for quite a few Christmases, but then she began to see it with enormous old cars out front and moving along the street. Eventually the cars began to look like something from movies about the 1950s and then they began to look sleeker and longer.

"Gauging by the cars, I think I'm coming up on the 1970s," she said, quietly. "Where are you?"

"I'm seeing maybe the late 1960s," Henry said. "Should we pick a Christmas and peek in?"

"Sure, let's try," Nona looked into the house and found it run down and filthy. She couldn't tell if anyone was living there, but clearly her grandparents had not yet moved in. She let a season pass and looked again, seeing it somewhat cleared out, but not yet inhabited. One Christmas later and she hit the jackpot. The house was clean, sparsely furnished but was clearly her grandparents'. The old piano she knew so well was sitting exactly where it would sit 40 years in the future and a few other odds and ends looked familiar to her as well.

"Look for an upright piano," Nona said. "The first year that the house has a piano should work."

"Okay," Henry said slowly, his voice sounding like someone who was working very hard at something. Perking up a bit he said, "I've got it."

At that moment, Nona gave a small gasp. "Henry, you're here. I can see your face. Stay put," she said excitedly.

She had just spotted Henry's face, dimly, in the room she was seeing just as she had spotted Director Walden when he Glimpsed her family. She was surprised at how much better she felt knowing he was there, even if only as a Glimpser. She began the process of mentally looking around the house. They were in luck in that no one appeared to be home. As they both concentrated on the house with all their energy, neither of them noticed that

Winnie had gone completely silent.

"I'm going to Travel," Nona said nervously. "Keep an eye out for anyone coming home, okay?" Henry gave a soft "uh-huh," which was Nona's cue to pull the pouch outside of the front of her dress and let herself leap. She felt tentative and realized that her fear of being discovered was causing her to pull back a bit as she passed through time. The result was a quiet, graceful landing right beside the piano.

"Oh, I see you," Henry said.

"I can still see your face, Henry. I'll get the money," Nona hurried to the hallway baseboard and jiggled it free, making as little noise as possible. She grinned when she saw the metal box. Taking a last look around, she pulled it out, opened it and thumbed through the money. The currency was arranged by year, so she quickly grabbed everything from 1898 and earlier, knowing Winnie couldn't travel any further forward in time than the date they had left her parents' farm. She snapped the box shut and put it back where she had found it.

"Don't forget the note," Henry whispered. Nona nodded and scribbled the words they had agreed upon on the message pad beside the phone, just a few feet from the piano. She closed up the box, slipped it in place and put the baseboard back. She stood up and turned to take a last look around and let out a startled, "Oh … how … "

Before she had a second to think, she was hurtling backwards through time, too shocked this time to slow down. She reappeared at Mesa Verde like a rocket, slamming into her two friends and knocking them over sideways into the dust and dirt of the cliff dwelling floor.

CHAPTER 15

"Winnie," Nona didn't realize she was shouting. "How on earth … I mean … you shouldn't be able to see the future, should you?"

"What?" Henry was pulling himself back into a sitting position and spitting out the dirt that had been ground into his mouth during Nona's return.

"I don't know what any of us should or should not be able to do, least of all myself," Winnie said, white faced with tears running down her cheeks. "I just followed your instructions. Then I started seeing things that didn't make any sense."

"What?" Henry had cleared the dirt from his mouth and had begun picking up the money that lay strewn all around them.

"Well of course you did," Nona could easily imagine Winnie's confusion based on her experiences in recent days. "But how? Can we all Glimpse the future? Is it one of your abilities but not one of ours? Is it something we're not even supposed to try to do? Did we do something wrong?"

"She Glimpsed the future?" Henry dropped the money he had been gathering, letting it fall into an untidy heap in front of him. "I thought we couldn't go forward." His eyes grew very wide as he turned to Nona. "Wait a minute, you could see her? Right. You could see me too. We can see when people Glimpse us?"

"No, not we, just me," Nona said distractedly. She was feeling woefully unprepared for what was going on around her. "My family told me that it's unusual to see Glimpsers. They said that sometimes Plodders see a Glimpser and think it's a ghost."

"But the future," Henry sounded agitated. "I thought you said we couldn't go to the future. If that's true then she shouldn't be able to see it either, should she?"

Nona felt herself slipping into something between helplessness and anger. She felt hot, slippery tears roll down her cheeks. Letting her head drop until her chin nearly touched her chest, she began to cry. As she sobbed, she realized she was crying for about a dozen reasons and knew she was going to have to get a grip and explain herself to her friends.

"I'm sorry," she said, pausing to hiccup and sniffle. "I don't suppose either of you have a Kleenex, do you?"

"A what?" Winnie asked, as she patted Nona's shoulder with a look of concern on her face.

"It's a disposable hankie," Henry said, adding, "Sorry, handkerchief," after glancing at Winnie's still bewildered face.

"No," Winnie said, fishing in a deep pocket in the side-seam of her skirt. "But I have this," with which she produced a lace-trimmed, white handkerchief that was embroidered with her initials in pink thread.

Nona nodded and took the hankie, thanking Winnie. Henry and Winnie muttered a few "It's going to be alright" and "Don't let yourself worry so much" sentences as Nona composed herself.

"I feel so helpless sometimes," Nona said, as she settled down. "I don't know enough about Traveling and what we can and can't do and what's allowed and not allowed. I'm worried about all of our families and I don't know what I'm supposed to do."

"This one is we," Henry said when she had finished. "It's what *we* should do, not just you. You sound as though you are supposed to be taking care of us. Nona, you've saved my life already. If you hadn't been in Winnie's barn at the moment I popped in, I would probably have bounced through time until I died."

"We are all Travelers, Nona," Winnie said with some pride in her voice. "You may know more about all of this than we do, but we don't expect you to know everything, and I am sorry if I have made you feel as though you should. We ask you questions because you're the only one of us that has even the faintest chance of knowing the answers."

"You're not responsible for us, but I'd like to think we are all responsible for each other," Henry said, accompanied by several nods of agreement from Winnie.

Nona took a deep, still-slightly-shaky breath and managed a bit of a smile for her friends. Looking at them, she felt terrifically grateful that she wasn't alone. "I'll tell you this for sure," she said, "I am going to pay incredible attention to everything my family has to tell me about Traveling when we're all back together."

As she looked at Winnie, she realized the girl looked pale and was frowning slightly. Nona felt immediately guilty that in her own outburst she had forgotten that Winnie had seen decades into the future of her world.

"Winnie, I can't imagine how strange the world must have looked to you," Nona said slowly. "When I arrived in your world, there were some confusing things to get used to, but I've seen films and TV shows that were set in your time, so it didn't look completely strange to me. Are you okay?"

Winnie nodded gravely and said, "I will be fine. There was just so much I had never seen before. I can't imagine I will live to see such things. But then I hear you two mention things, such as seeing these … things," she fluttered her hands with a look of frustration on her face, "that were set in my time. I realize you understand your times, but you also understand my time. I don't even know the names for much of what I saw in the future." She sighed. "It is all just a bit overwhelming."

"You know," Henry said, sounding a little distracted as he went back to sorting the money Nona had brought with her. "I never thought about this before, but films and TV shows are set in the future sometimes, or what someone imagines the future to be. So anyone who lives in the 1950s or later would have some ideas about what the future might look like. I wonder if any of the people writing those films and shows about the future are Travelers who might have seen the future?"

They sat in silence for a bit, all of them sorting money and pursuing their own thoughts. Once they had it sorted by country of origin and then by year, they decided to use Mesa Verde as a bank of sorts. The question was where to put it. They couldn't risk letting the Wetherills find the Anasazi dwellings in the coming year, only to discover a pile of currency from their past and ten years into their future.

"I know where to put it," Nona blurted, startling the other two, who were silently stewing about a safe storage place. "There's a dwelling on the far west side of the park, called Mug House, that won't be discovered until some terrible fires go through here during my time. It's pretty hard to get to, which means a long, hard hike, but I'm very sure no one will find anything we leave in it. Let's put it all there for now and plan on coming back to this place and time after we get a look at the message. Once we're back here, we'll figure out what to do and get whatever money we may need. Sound good?"

The others agreed immediately, but as they began collecting the tidy stacks of ornate currency, Henry paused and said, "Maybe we should Travel there and back instead of hiking, so that we can practice controlling our arrivals. We came somersaulting in here like a bunch of amateur gymnasts and, no offense Nona, but your last return wasn't exactly ballet either. Sooner or later we're going to get hurt, destroy something or give away our location if we don't get a little more graceful."

The girls had to laugh at this and agree with it too. Nona had hiked to the dwelling several times, but even so, it took a long while and a lot of looking to pick it out of the thick brush that had grown up around it and over the trail leading to it.

"Henry, that's a great idea," Nona said. "It would have taken us an eternity to hike there and it would have been pretty treacherous in spots."

Even Glimpsing the little cliff dwelling proved tricky, but eventually Nona found it. The trio linked arms and Traveled back one week to the smaller dwelling. Henry devised a little cache, using tumbled down rocks to secure the currency from curious animals. After several trips back and forth from Cliff Palace to Mug House, they began to feel quite confident about their ability to control their arrivals.

"Shall we go and find the quilt?" Nona asked, after they had rested a bit and eaten the last of the food they had on hand. She had enjoyed the jaunts to Mug House more than she had expected. Each time she Traveled, she felt more certain that she would actually get to where and when she was going, which helped lessen her fears for herself and her friends. But seeing Mug House in this time was particularly special for her. Like the rest of what would be Mesa Verde National Park, the canyon over which the little dwelling presided was completely still. There were no sounds of cars, planes or tourists. She chuckled a bit to herself, thinking that in her own time Mug House was still almost silent, but there was something thrilling in breathing the pristine sage and juniper-scented air that hadn't yet been tainted by car, bus and RV exhaust. It was also a bit sobering to know that the silence and isolation of the ruin extended for miles upon miles in all directions.

"Let's do it," Henry said with an encouraging smile. "Let's go find the message and figure out what to do next." Winnie nodded, her face somewhat less eager than Henry's.

"We need a good plan," Henry said, rubbing his hands together. Winnie and Nona looked at each other and smiled.

"Henry," Winnie said, "You do enjoy a good plan."

"Well, yeah, I do," he said, sounding a little miffed. "Let's say we get separated going to look for the message. If we haven't made a plan for that contingency, we will panic and we may never find each other again. I don't think that's anything to make fun of."

"Oh no," Winnie sounded stricken, "I wasn't making sport. I just meant that you are always the one to organize and make a plan. It's as though that's part of your job as we Travel."

"It's true, Henry," Nona added. "We are each stronger at some things than others and one of your strengths is clearly laying out plans."

Henry seemed to feel better with those explanations and returned to the plan. "What if we agree to meet at Mug House here at Mesa Verde, later this afternoon? We know today is the fourth of June in 1888. Let's shoot to meet on the fourth of July 1888. It should be an easy day to spot as we're Glimpsing, what with parades and fireworks and all. We know we won't be there after this morning, nor will anyone else."

Nona and Winnie contemplated Henry's logic for a moment before beginning to nod.

"I think that's a good plan," Nona said, knowing full well that the conversation was more about comfort than about an actual working arrangement. "We have the pouches which should help, but we don't really know if Henry can control his Traveling yet or if Winnie can Travel alone at all. I think we have to be really aware of sticking together at all times. We can never be in a bad situation and be more than a few steps apart – agreed?"

"I would certainly prefer that," Winnie said, with a frown.

"Don't worry, Winnie, we're not going to lose each other," Henry said grinning at her. Nona had stopped smiling.

"No," she said abruptly. "We just don't know enough about either of your abilities yet. We aren't comfortable having either of you try to get to Mug House on your own from here and now, what makes us think it's going to work from another time and place?" She was shaking her head so vigorously that it was giving her a dull headache. "This is too dangerous."

She looked up to see Henry purse his lips and frown. She hoped it was a thoughtful expression, not an angry one, but she couldn't tell. Winnie let out a deep sigh that sounded to Nona like the sort of sound her father might make when terribly worried about something.

After a few minutes of silence, Henry sat up straight and blurted, "We can do a redo!"

"I beg your pardon," Winnie said, with a bit of an edge in her voice.

"A redo," he said, sounding a little impatient. "If we screw up somehow, Nona can go back in time and tell one of us not to make the trip so that we don't get separated. That way we should get to this moment with the knowledge that whatever we tried the first time didn't work. We'll know what not to do. Right?"

Nona stared at Henry for a moment and then let her gaze drop absently to the dirt floor as she thought his idea through. After a few moments of stewing about it she looked up at her partners.

"I think that should work. I know I can get here on this day, so if something happens I'll just come back to Mesa Verde and talk to one of you two this morning, before I wake up. Or would that be woke up?" She paused and shook her head. "You know what I mean. Does that make any sense?"

No one moved or spoke at first. Finally Winnie began to nod.

"That's the ticket," Henry said, sounding enthusiastic. "That feels like a safer plan than mine, I have to admit. Let's do it."

Nona took a moment to take a few deep, relaxing breaths before saying, "I think the way to do this is going to be really similar to the way we got here," Nona said, looking at both Winnie and Henry to make sure she had their attention. "I'll Glimpse the old quilt at my grandparents' house and see if I can use it to see the sod house again. Once I see it, I'll tell you. You two hang on to me and we'll go. Okay?"

Nona's friends scooted over to sit right beside her, one on either side, and looped their arms in hers. Henry and Winnie both turned their heads to face Nona, looking at her with serious looks of concentration, and Nona pulled her anchor pouch from inside her dress so it was no longer touching her skin.

"Pull your pouches out right before we go," she instructed, before closing her eyes and letting herself take what now felt like a familiar path through time and space to Glimpse her grandparents' house in what should be her present time. As the living room came into view, Nona wondered why she always came back to that part of the house. Perhaps because it was where she had been when Hildie had tossed the quilt at her to send her hurtling to Winnie's farm? Or maybe it was because that was where she had last seen her family.

The room was quiet and still in a complete disarray. Baxter was nowhere to be found, although Nona knew he had a cat door to the outside and had a good friend in the elderly woman who lived next door. He was not going hungry, she was sure. But something was not quite right. It took Nona a good couple of minutes of looking around to realize that several things had been moved since she had last seen the room. Winnie's quilt and the Tootsie Roll sign were both sitting in the middle of the dining room table, as though someone had handled them and set them down there. The quilt was folded neatly, the sign leaning against it.

As Nona realized what was out of place in the scene in front of her, she heard the sounds of someone rummaging vigorously through a drawer in one of the second-floor bedrooms. Tentatively, more than a little afraid of what she might find, Nona moved her concentration to the second floor, where she paused to listen, but the sound had stopped. Nona held her breath, Glimpsing slowly along the upstairs hallway and pausing in front of her grandparents' bedroom door. She was about to peer in when a young man, probably in his twenties and nicely dressed in a suit and tie, popped out of the guest room and came straight down the hall toward her. Nona tried to move out of the way, but was so startled that she hesitated a moment too long. He passed right through her, taking one more step before freezing in his tracks.

Her heart hammering in her chest, Nona turned to look at him as he too turned around slowly. He appeared to stare right into her face. Horrified, Nona moved slightly to the right, out of the line of his gaze. His eyes didn't follow her. He reached up a hand and swiped the air where Nona had been a moment earlier. He began taking wider swipes up and down the hallway, but Nona had already ducked into the guest room and was keeping an eye on him from well inside the cluttered room. After two passes up and down the hallway, looking more frightened and angry with each step, the young man turned on his heel and raced down the stairs. Nona moved into the hallway to watch him, just in time to see him glance toward the living room before disappearing with a wet, popping sound. She could hear a hum that decrescendoed as he left, something she had never heard before. Somehow she knew he had taken a path to SOOT, although she didn't know how or why she knew that.

Nona waited for a minute or more, listening to make sure no one else was in the house and trying to place the man's face. She felt as though she had seen him, or maybe a younger version of him, somewhere. He looked like someone she had met, but she couldn't place him. Finally assured that the house was empty, Nona turned and began Glimpsing her way toward the guest room and the old quilt.

"Oh, my gosh," Nona repeated several times, her heart racing again. She knew where she had seen him. It had not been a younger version of him that she had met, it had been an older version. She had either met him 20 years later in his life, or had met his father, when that man Glimpsed her family and then Visited, just before she was sent to Winnie's. He was a younger version of the director, or he was the son of the director.

Nona ignored distant, worried questions from Henry and Winnie as she hurried her attention back to the guest room. She saw Winnie's mother's quilt on the bed, although tangled into a rumpled pile rather than folded, as it had been. After a nervous glance around the room and another back toward the hallway, to assure there was no one there, Nona turned her attention to the quilt. She let the guest room fade to a blur and focused on the growing image of the sod house with its oddly-lumpy walls. The images were hazier than they had been in her other Glimpses. Logically, she decided, it made sense that Glimpsing within a Glimpse would be a little different than what she had grown accustomed to in the past few days, if logic could be applied to Glimpsing in the first place. Nona moved her attention around the little sod house and found no one home. Looking out the windows, she saw no one in the farmyard either.

Concentrating with all her might, Nona said "Hang on" to her friends and felt them tighten their grips on her arms. She relaxed and let the past tug her through time to the farmhouse she was Glimpsing, her friends pressed close to her sides. The rush of sounds, smells and little flashes of strange places and events still startled her. Judging by the way Winnie and Henry were gripping her arms, she knew they felt the same way. She saw the now-familiar room of the sod house ahead of her, as though at the end of a quickly shortening tunnel. Leaning back to slow down their arrival, she managed to bring them in relatively smoothly, although they all managed to trip over each other's feet, stumbling and falling to the floor the moment they arrived.

CHAPTER 16

"Smooth," Henry whispered, as he struggled to pull his leg out from under Nona's knees.

"Remember, we have got to stick together," Nona cautioned, examining every corner of the room for people or Glimpsers. She had an uneasy feeling that whoever was in her grandparents' house when she Glimpsed it might be able to find them.

"What happened back there?" Winnie asked, hanging onto Nona's skirt as they all looked around the room. Henry had let go, but was staying no more than a foot from Nona. "You looked really worried."

"I'll explain later," Nona said tersely. "Let's go look at the quilt, figure out what Aunt Hildie's message is and get out of here."

Moving without getting more than a step away from each other, as though they were drawn together by magnets, the three friends made their way to the bedroom, stumbling occasionally on each other's feet along the way. The quilt lay on the bed, half of it covered by a plain white sheet.

"I wonder why someone covered it up," Nona said aloud.

"To protect it from the sun," Winnie answered.

Henry reached out as though to touch it, only to jump back when Nona called out a sharp, "No! That's an old quilt. Your skin oils can damage it."

Winnie giggled slightly before saying, "Nona, it won't be an antique for a long time. Right now it's a new quilt that holds a message for us."

The voice that sounded from the doorway behind them couldn't have frightened them more if it had been the blast of a train whistle. All three Travelers jumped and turned to face the door, which wouldn't have been a problem, had they not been standing so close together. They bumped into each other, staggered and fell to the floor before any of them actually got a good look at who had spoken. Henry, with no skirts and petticoats to deal with, was the first to his feet. Nona saw him raise his fists in a fierce defensive posture and heard the person in the doorway speak again.

"Henry, don't worry," said the oddly-familiar voice. " I'm so sorry to have frightened you."

It was Winnie who did the math first, quietly asking, "Mother? Is that you?"

The person in the doorway was a teenaged version of Winnie's mother, Nona suddenly realized, and was staring hard at Winnie. Nona got to her feet and helped the stunned Winnie to her feet as well. Henry brought his arms down, but kept his fists balled up. He had the look of a cat that was tensed to pounce at any moment.

"The message isn't in the quilt," the young version of Winnie's mother said, obviously having difficulty tearing her eyes from the daughter she wouldn't meet for years to come. Looking at Nona, she said, "It's in me, or rather she told it to me. She said you wouldn't have much time and that I should tell you everything quickly." Nona nodded, feeling a little more worried by the idea of not having much time.

"Your Aunt Hildie said that she, your parents and your grandparents are fine. They are not together, but they Glimpse and speak daily. She said that men from SOOT, young men, ransacked your grandparents' house and you should not go back there again because it seems as though it's being monitored."

Nona frowned, wondering if it was possible for whoever was monitoring the house to follow her back to Mesa Verde or here, for that matter. She looked around, nervously, as the girl in the doorway continued.

"The young men from SOOT seemed to be looking for something specific, or perhaps several specific things, but she doesn't know yet what those things might be. She doesn't know if they are the thieves that have been taking artifacts from SOOT or if they think your grandparents are the thieves, but she doesn't want to tangle with them yet and neither should you." The girl paused, taking a deep breath.

Nona nodded, hoping she would come up with some good news or at least something helpful.

"She said that nothing anyone is doing these days conforms to SOOT protocols and laws, so it's hard to tell the good people from the bad ones. She said not to go to SOOT under any circumstances. Don't even Glimpse it." The girl who one day would be Winnie's mother raised her eyebrows and Nona nodded that she understood.

The young Aunt Edith was about to continue when Henry interrupted her, saying, "Excuse me, but I think we should be keeping an eye out for anyone who might come to the house." He looked at Nona for agreement. She nodded and he stepped past Aunt Edith and began moving from window to window, taking time at each one to scan the yard and the far horizon before moving on. Winnie, meanwhile, couldn't take her eyes off of the young version of her mother and was taking small, hesitant steps toward her.

Edith continued, "Hildie told me to tell you that you will be safest in crowded places in times of great turmoil. Apparently it's harder to sense Travelers when there are a lot of people about and their emotions are running high. She also said … " She stopped talking in response to Nona's raised hand.

Nona tilted her head for a brief moment and then went pale, shouting, "Traveler coming this way fast!"

The next few seconds were a blur of Winnie tearing her eyes from her young mother and turning toward Nona with a bewildered look and Henry charging into the room at a trot, shouting "Let's go."

Nona closed her eyes to help herself imagine Mesa Verde, which meant she wasn't at all braced for what happened next. She would find out later that Henry grabbed Winnie's shoulders as he ran into the room and propelled her in Nona's direction, following right behind her and not letting go. Nona, who didn't see them coming, was taken off guard when the two of them bumped into her with a fair amount of momentum. Her eyes flew open as she stumbled backwards, flailing her arms to find something to steady herself.

Nona felt the edge of a chair with the back of her legs as she fell backwards. She dimly remembered a frail wooden chair sitting against the wall with some sort of vase full of weedy-looking flowers sitting on it, as though to keep a person from sitting and crushing it.

Three people careening together onto the fragile chair was more than the old wood could take. It collapsed with a dry splitting sound, quickly joined by the splattering and crashing of the vase full of flowers hitting the floor. Nona's hand came to rest on a chunk of splintered wood as she fell to the floor, with Winnie and Henry falling on top of her.

Only they didn't stop moving when they hit the floor. Nona felt the familiar tug of Travel, combined with the moment of falling and knew they were in for rough ride. Reaching out in a panic, she grabbed Winnie's arm and Henry's foot and tried to lean away from the direction in which they were moving in hopes of slowing them down. But the momentum of the fall was too much to fight and all she could do was brace herself for their arrival in whatever time and place they were heading toward.

***

The arrival wasn't good. The trio landed on dusty, hard-packed dirt in a somersaulting, rolling tangle of arms, legs, skirts and petticoats. Nona lost her grip on her friends as she skidded to a stop in bright sunlight that was blinding in comparison to the dim room they had left behind. She heard Henry and

Winnie sputtering and spitting dirt as she did the same thing herself.

As her eyes adjusted to the bright sunlight, Nona saw an open wagon holding several chairs just like the one they had just shattered at the farmhouse. Looking around beyond the wagon, she began to panic. They had landed in the middle of what appeared to be a town square. Surrounding the trio of disheveled Travelers were small clusters of terrified looking people, all of whom were dressed in black with wide, white collars of various shapes. Most of them were inching backwards with their hands clasped over their mouths. Nona had a fleeting thought that the clothing looked familiar somehow, as she scrambled to her knees and began to crawl toward her companions. But her knees and feet got tangled in her skirt and she fell flat on her face again. When she tried a second time, pulling up her skirts to give herself more freedom of movement, she heard a chorus of screams.

"Witches!" came a cry from a single voice in the crowd, followed by a chorus of people shouting the same word. The shouts confirmed Nona's worst fears. They had landed in the middle of Salem, Massachusetts, in what had to be the era of the Salem witch trials. The clothing looked familiar from a documentary on the era that her class had watched a few months earlier.

"Henry, Winnie, this is bad! We've got to get out of here," she called to her friends, then a sharp blow from something not altogether hard hit the middle of her back and knocked her flat again. Several men descended on the three Travelers, whacking them with everything from brooms, which Nona saw was what had just hit her, to canes and what looked like some sort of long whips. The men dragged Nona, Winnie and Henry, who were each kicking, flailing madly, in three different directions. Nona could hear frightened screams and whimpers from Winnie and angry shouts from Henry. She realized she was shouting too. But she knew no one was listening.

Nona lost sight of her friends as she was half dragged, half carried to a small wooden shed. She was bound, wrists and ankles tied together with thick, coarse rope, and then tossed unceremoniously through the door, which was then wedged in place from the outside. She heard men's voices speaking a variation of English that was full of words like "thee," "thou" and "prithee." From what she could gather, the men were posting guards around her shed and sending all of the women to barricade themselves in their homes.

Nona shimmied herself into an upright position, which wasn't easy given the rope that was beginning to cut off the blood flow to her feet and hands. Sitting in the dark on the little building's dirt floor, she shivered in fear. Her shoulder hurt enough that she thought it might be seriously injured. Her lip was split and bleeding from her face hitting the ground during their arrival and she was more frightened than she had ever been in her life. Trying to calm her mind, Nona concentrated on what she knew to be fact about their situation. She was certain she knew where and when they were. The clothing of the people in the square combined with a tangy sea and fish odor and the smells of wood smoke, food cooking and horse manure all mingled to confirm her first thoughts.

Nona decided to use Henry's approach to problems and make a plan. First, she would untie her hands and feet. Several minutes of working on the knots at her wrists with her teeth made her abandon that plan. Rethinking, she decided that their plan for an emergency was the only thing she could do to help her friends. She had to go back to Mesa Verde and warn either Winnie or Henry about falling on the old chair in the sod farmhouse and where it would send them. The only way out of this mess was to avoid getting into it, as far as she could see. But going to Mesa Verde meant leaving her friends behind in a time and place she wasn't certain she could return to, which felt terribly wrong.

She reminded herself that staying here and doing nothing was also terribly wrong, since she was the only one who could help Winnie and Henry right now. The realization that her friends were depending on her to leave and keep them from coming to Salem in the first place was enough to jar her into action.

Nona closed her eyes, took several deep breaths and began to visualize Mesa Verde on the morning she had awoken to find herself alone in the little cliff dwelling room. Henry had been somewhere out in the canyon, she recalled, exploring and foraging. Winnie had been quietly exploring the cliff dwelling.

She saw Cliff Palace clearly and then saw Winnie picking her way carefully up a tumble of rocks to peer into one of the dwelling's many doorways. She began to hear Winnie muttering softly to herself and was just about to Travel when a blood-curdling scream jerked her back to the reality of the dark little space in which she was confined. Winnie! Nona heard heavy footsteps rushing toward her little prison and heard men's voices shouting in what sounded like fear.

Nona heard the door brace kicked aside and saw a blinding flash of sunlight as the door opened. She heard more screaming from outside the building and saw a flash of light behind her as the men crowding through the door began to emit their own screams. One of the men swung something long and wooden in Nona's general direction, connecting fairly solidly with the side of her head. She heard the thud of wood connecting with her skull but felt no pain as everything went hopelessly dark and silent.

***

Lavender. Nona was aware of a light scent of lavender creeping into a dreamless sleep. She drifted awhile, enjoying the scent as well as the feel of soft cotton against her skin. Several minutes passed before she began to remember where she was and what was happening. She jerked awake with a shout, tensing against her restraints. But the rope was gone and her arms flew up over her head and smacked into some cold metals bars. The combination of shock at the freedom of movement, the pain in her shoulder and wrists and the fact she had just opened her eyes to find herself in a dimly-lit bedroom, tucked into an old-fashioned brass bed made her scream and struggle to free herself from the sheets and blankets tucked around her.

"Nona," came a familiar voice from the hall, followed by several more familiar voices and the sound of running footsteps. Her father came through the door first, a grave, worried look on his face. Her mother and her grandparents followed on his heels, with Hildie bringing up the rear. Unable to control the combination of fear and relief she felt, Nona burst into tears. She knew she was babbling through her sobs, but she had to tell them about Winnie and Henry.

Her parents were trying to stop her struggling and flailing, while her grandmother was gathering up the blankets that she kicked away and Hildie was gathering up what appeared to be medical supplies. As was their style, they were all talking at once. "Quiet," her grandfather yelled over the top of all of this, his voice silencing them and putting a stop to Nona's struggling. "They're safe," he said in a calm voice.

"Henry and Winnie are here, in rooms down the hall," he said calmly, looking Nona squarely in the eyes as he spoke. "They are both asleep, or at least they were until this mayhem erupted. You're all a little worse for wear."

In the moments of quiet that followed, Nona allowed Hildie to check the bandages taped in place on her wrists and ankles. She realized she was wearing a soft, white cotton nightgown and that she didn't recognize the room around her at all. She heard what sounded like row boats, complete with creaking, gently splashing oars, outside the open French windows and was quite certain she heard people speaking French out there as well. She was just beginning to take stock of the old-fashioned clothing her family members were wearing, from shirts without collars and suspenders on her dad and grandfather to long skirts and buttoned-up, long-sleeved blouses on her mother, aunt and grandmother.

"How … where?" Nona waffled between questions.

"You're in Paris, sweetie," her grandmother told her, sitting down on the newly smoothed quilts on the bed. Nona saw the quilts and reached up for her pouch, relieved at finding one tucked under her nightgown. "Don't worry, I made one for each of you when we got here."

"The year is 1910," her father said, taking a chair beside the bed and looking as close to tears as Nona had ever seen him. "We knew something had happened at the house, so we Visited Edith about a year after the three of you had been there. She told us that the three of you had shattered the old chair and disappeared from her house. That chair had been in the family since they arrived on this continent in 1692. We knew straight away where you had gone."

"It just took us a little while to figure out exactly when and where you arrived," her mother said, sitting on the bed beside Nona and smoothing her daughter's hair as she spoke. "We Glimpsed until we located all three of you and then we all Traveled at once and grabbed you."

Her grandfather, pacing at the foot of the bed, said, "We'll fix the historical mess we've created in Salem later. What's important is that the three of you are safe now."

Hildie, who Nona didn't realize had left the room until she stepped back in, said, "Amazingly, they're both still sleeping like babies."

"Were they hurt?" Nona asked, a little afraid of the answer. "I heard a terrible scream right before … well, before I woke up here."

"They're a little banged up, but they're not hurt any worse than you are," Hildie said, reaching over the footboard to pat Nona's leg. "That scream you heard was Winnie. She was a bit alarmed by our arrival."

Nona smiled thinking of Winnie's likely reaction to seeing the unannounced appearance of distant relatives from her future. Pulling her lips into a smile hurt, which reminded her of her split lip. She was about to ask what her family had found out in the days they had been apart from her, when the sound of two row boats smacking together and angry curses in French distracted her.

"Are we on a lake?" she asked.

"No," Hildie said, walking to the window to peer down at the commotion below. "We are in an apartment building not far from the River Seine in the middle of the great Paris flood of 1910."

"The city is in a complete palaver," her father explained. "The streets are flooded all over this part of town. People are using row boats to get around the streets and a lot of them are treating it as a great celebration of some sort."

"Did you get our message about times of great upheaval?" Hildie asked. Nona nodded. "Well this is one of them. I keep an apartment in this time as a safe house. I have several others, in other times, which I'll tell you about later. The commotion and disruption all over the city makes it nearly impossible for anyone to track a Traveler in this time and place."

Nona nodded again, but felt her eyelids growing heavy as she did so.

"Everybody out," her grandfather decreed in a gentle voice. "Let's let her sleep for now. In fact, we should all get some sleep. We're safe for the moment, but there's a lot to be dealt with ahead of us."

Nona was nearly asleep by the time everyone had taken turns kissing her forehead, adjusting the quilts and tiptoeing out of the room. Safe for the moment, she thought, wondering just what a moment really meant for a Traveler.

ABOUT THE AUTHOR

Elaine Schmidt is the author of *Hey Mom! Listen to This!: A Parent's Guide to Music* (Hal Leonard, 2010) and *All About Singing* (Hal Leonard, 2011). She has worked as a writer, arranger, translator and editor on more than 100 music publications for the Hal Leonard Corporation, G. Schirmer, and Ricordi. She lives in the Milwaukee area where she writes regularly about classical music, dance and theater for *Milwaukee Journal Sentinel.* Ms. Schmidt has written for *Current Musicology, Back Stage, Opera Canada, Music Express, American Record Guide, Dance Teacher* and other arts magazines and has scripted and hosted numerous arts broadcasts on Milwaukee Public Television. Trained as a flutist and singer, Ms. Schmidt spent more than a decade performing throughout North America before she began writing about the arts. She holds an undergraduate degree in music and an MA in Music Criticism.